A Time to Reap

Therèse Tappouni

A Time to Reap

Original cover art, *Seal Woman*, a watercolor by Therèse Tappouni
Author's photo: Rob Mason, Lucid Productions, Hollywood, CA
Editor: Lance Ware

ISBN: 0-9705500-2-2

Distribution: NBN/Biblio

Published by
Whole Heart Publishing

19841 Gulf Blvd.
Indian Shores, FL 33785

Tel: 727.593.3757
Fax: 727.593.9253

www.wholeheart.net

Previous Works

Lot's Wife, Skin Drum Press, 1994

Night Gardening: Passionate Poems for the Beloved, (with Lance Ware), Whole Heart Publishing, 2000

Walking Your Walk: A Woman's Guide to a Spirit Filled Life, Whole Heart Publishing, 2000

For Michael, who taught each of us.

"All that we will take across the waters of Death is the jewel of love."

Rumi

Acknowledgments

To my greatest life gift, my children Michelle, Michael, Paul, Catherine, Christopher, and Mary for their love and patience.

And to Lance Ware, my life partner and writing partner, who surprised me in the fullness of my world. Not only for his presence, his love and his life but for his incredible editing of this manuscript.

To a special circle of women who never doubted and lifted me on a lake of loving support. There are more than I can name, but they are still here. For my chosen sisters Alice, Pat, Chris and Kathi, life healers, Katie, Jill and Jan, my daughters, my sisters, and my mother, who now knows the answers to questions we are still asking.

And to Jim McKinley, a wonderful teacher at UMKC, who saw the potential of the short story that was to become this book.

And to the gracious and talented group at TurnKey Press who brought my vision to life.

Prologue

The scent of seaweed rose from his shoulders, and all around them mist and fog drifted in the candlelight. Their skin wore delicate drops of moisture. His hands knew her, had sculpted her from stone, and she lifted toward him with a cry of recognition born in a long ago time. His cry matched hers, floating out of the garden and joining the calls of seabirds riding the Pacific currents.

Later, he covered her with a blanket from his studio. He stroked her hair, her face. Neither spoke but fell into dreamless sleep curled into each other.

*****

The next morning, Maureen awoke to the sounds of birds and the smell of coffee and biscuits. She would meditate near the water and hold this to herself for a while longer. The usual wisps of mist blew across the windows as she slipped into a sweater and out the back door, the sensations of joy and satisfaction flooding her like warm brandy. Her body seemed to walk ahead, unaware of the light rain or the clouds lowering on the horizon. The temperature dropped, but Maureen walked in a cocoon of sunshine.

The fog thickened as she neared the ocean, the surf booming far below. She looked around, puzzled, her smile fading. She must have missed the path. The fog swirled at her feet, parted briefly to reveal the rocky coast, then closed again. She heard a muffled voice calling, but the fog tricked the ear so she couldn't tell which direction it was coming from. She'd better go back to the lodge. Brigit had warned them about how quickly the fog could move in, but she wouldn't have been able to imagine this. She turned back the way she thought she had come, and the earth opened underneath her. She hit her head as she slid through the jagged rocks, felt herself flung like a rag doll into the freezing whirlpool below. Some part of her remembered she hadn't told Brigit about the break in the cliff. She could hear her name as the water closed over her head, the pain erased in the ice-blue cold. She heard the voice pleading for her to stop and wait for him.

She was falling but without fear, lightly, as if she had wings. The frigid water turned her blood to shards of crystal, piercing her heart, before the surf pulled her out and under, into a soothing blue warmth. She felt solid, sleek, and powerful as she spiraled deeper. Others escorted her descent, their skin gleaming in the purple light cutting through the midnight waters. Her breathing was one with the water, the rocks, the seals that called to her in their mournful human voices. She gave up to the unknown, floating alone into a familiar cave, her eyes flared like anemones. The walls of the cave trembled and leaned inward as the tide surged, licking up the rocks like tongues of cold fire. A whirlpool pulled her backwards, swirled her toward the entrance that was slowly filling with the tide. It was then that she saw him suspended in front of her, the water around him shimmering, his long hair caressing the tenderness of his neck and shoulders.

Chapter One

Maureen pushed open the heavy wooden door of the Church of the Immaculate Conception. Incense, heavy as guilt, spilled over her. Awash in the past, she entered the church that pulled her every year on a day in January, the date her son had been buried nearly seventeen years ago. She didn't find Dylan here, but the small side altar where the Virgin held out her arms was her touchstone. No matter how far she swam from her Catholicism, the image of the compassionate mother was her spiritual buoy. She lit a blue candle and knelt, leaning into the railing as the echoes of past visits whispered in the dome above the main altar. The pain of her loss knocked beneath her heart, but she was well schooled in the methods of containment. Only so much was allowed. The terror of fully experiencing her grief was second nature. She knew what she could and couldn't do. She didn't go to the cemetery, her last contact with Dylan. She came here, to this place where the pain of generations had been laid at the feet of one who knew. And she was comforted, if only for the moment.

But today was not that anniversary. Such a strange name, anniversary. Today was the day Maureen felt her control slipping. After all these years, her other two children were going away to college. Awareness of the void they would leave in her carefully organized life drifted to the surface with every shirt she bought for Bryan or when she heard Gabi on the phone with her friends talking about her first football date in Gainesville. The second skin on her heart was stretched like the skin on her belly just before a child was born. But this skin wasn't stretching, it was splitting. Her prayer today was simple. She asked only to hold on until Gabi and Bryan were gone. She prayed that they went with free hearts, believing their mother was fine and looking forward to birthing her new life.

"Give me strength," she prayed silently, looking up at the statue that represented what was left of her spiritual life.

Heat seared her body without warning, as it had been doing for some weeks. Sweat trickled between her breasts, an unfamiliar vertigo causing her to hold tight to the railing. The statue seemed to sway on its pedestal, and the right hand lifted toward Maureen. She froze in the midst of the radiating heat, watching the look of compassion on the face of the Virgin change to one of warning. And then she heard a voice, a voice that reverberated inside her rib cage. There were no words, but Maureen understood what she had been given. She would give birth one more time. This time, she would birth herself. She would need strength and courage. She couldn't stop what was about to happen.

Two weeks passed like moments and August drew to a close. The color of the Bermuda grass had drained into the earth in search of moisture, and the yard resembled the plains of Africa. Gabi and Bryan closed the doors of the U-Haul, got in the car, and were gone. Just like that. No drum roll, no ritual. Just gone. The dry blades scratched Maureen's feet as she waved at her life disappearing down Martinique Drive. Both of them going to Gainesville to the University of Florida, leaving her childless for the first time in nearly twenty-three years. She stood a long while in the pitiless Florida sun until she grew dizzy visualizing Gabi's Honda speeding up Interstate 75, rock music trailing behind, littering the highway like confetti. For Gabi and Bryan, it was a celebration of independence. She stumbled as she climbed the porch steps.

In the quiet house, Maureen heard the blood moving in her veins, a thick shushing that got louder by the second. She sat on the living room couch, hypnotized by the front door still vibrating with departure, and imagined her blood draining out on the cotton fabric like a Dali painting.

Silence pressed against her buzzing ears, a heavy silence that flowed down the walls and over the piano. She could barely breathe. She had to move or become the Lot's wife of Tampa, looking forever backwards.

In the kitchen, she poured a glass of tea from her grandmother's hyacinth pitcher. She stood at the sliding doors that led into the backyard, watching sunlight glint off the surface of the pool. She closed her eyes against the glare, her mind against the vision. There was no pool, had been no pool in her yard for seventeen years. Not since Dylan ... She remembered the bulldozers filling in the hole, like a mass grave.

Frantic for reality, she took up her familiar copy of *The Joy of Cooking* and leafed through the splotched pages. Again, out of the corner of her eye, the sparkle of water. She squinted into the sun, willing the patio to be there. Instead, in the shimmer of heat, she conjured Dylan running through the backyard, waving behind him at the retreating school bus. She imagined his feet skidding on the wet pool deck, a surprised look crossing his small face as he hit the edge of the pool and slid in, blood blooming around him like ink.

The door to Maureen's memory slammed shut. The patio and oak trees reappeared, and she was in her kitchen holding a shattered glass, blood dripping on her recipe for marinara sauce. Dazed, she washed her hand, drying it on a kitchen towel. She held the cut tight with her thumb and went to the bathroom for a bandage, her stomach turning at the sight of the slow spreading circle of red on her skirt. In the bathroom, she avoided the mirror, pulling the jagged edges of her cut together with a butterfly tape, then cleaning the area with peroxide. As the water carried her blood down the drain, she cleared her mind of the pool and the manufactured memory of the exact moment of Dylan's death. After all, she hadn't been there.

Maureen awoke a half hour later on the couch in the den, her head dull and cottony. As she sat up, she caught a glimpse of herself in the mirror over the mantle. Next to her on the floor was a bloody towel. Four o'clock, only hours since the kids had left and long before Jason would return from work. What now? She remembered the cookbook and went into the kitchen.

She splashed water on her hot face. She knew how to handle this: organization, lists, goals. Only now, the goals would be hers, not the children's.

Maureen closed the cookbook, concealing the bloodstained pages. She'd fix an elegant dinner for two. Maybe she and Jason could reclaim the couple they'd been before the kids came along. Maureen wrote down the ingredients for a sauce she'd made a thousand times, wrote down *one pound fettuccine* on her list. Today, she couldn't trust her memory. Jason loved caesar salad. She added anchovies and bread for croutons. Already she was feeling better.

Upstairs, she applied lip gloss, careful not to look at herself. She pulled on a clean cotton skirt, wadding up the bloody one and stuffing it behind the hamper, along with the kitchen towel. In the garage, heat sucked the breath from her lungs, the vinyl seats of the van searing her thighs. Sweat soaked the back of her blouse as she backed onto the street. The air conditioner struggled, blowing hot air into her face. She shut out the thoughts of Bryan and Gabi driving off to Gainesville, mentally adding fresh mushrooms to her list as she pulled into the parking lot.

Inside, she breathed deeply of the frigid air, inhaling in front of the green peppers as the automatic mister sprayed their shiny green skins fresh as a morning garden. She squeezed the eggplants and Italian tomatoes. She sniffed the fresh earth still clinging to the parsley, rubbed the oregano leaves between her fingers, releasing their sharp fragrance. Lingering at the bakery, she finally chose a still warm Italian loaf.

She drove home, then carried the chilled bags from the garage to her kitchen. Reds, greens, and the beauty of purple eggplant spilled onto her white marble pastry counter. She tied an apron around her waist, slid in a Maria Callas CD, singing along on the lower parts. She kept a reverent silence when that winged voice soared into the upper ranges. Even in Maureen's best days as a music major, Callas was the untouchable unreachable. She was perfection. The glorious notes floated around the kitchen, dropping into the steaming pots. While the sauce simmered, she ironed the linen tablecloth, a whiff of her childhood in Illinois rising from the border her grandmother had embroidered. Grandmother Quinn, sitting in her green upholstered chair with the rioting roses, knitting, embroidering, crocheting. She had died sitting up in that chair, a gossamer white blanket for her first great-grandchild taking shape in her lap.

She tucked the memory of her grandmother back in its special place, one of the few memories of childhood that made her smile and feel the warmth of love. She took the cloth into the dining room, spreading it carefully on the table. She'd never used it when the kids were at home, fearful that the delicate hues of tiny leaves and lily-of-the-valley would be ruined.

At six o'clock, Maureen set the table with the rarely used wedding crystal and china, opened the red wine and filled a glass for herself. She sipped it slowly, finishing the last drops in a rose scented bath. Jason rarely came home before eight, so she took her time, brushing her thick red hair back the way he liked it. She slipped into a simple yellow dress, turning quickly in front of the mirror. She never looked at herself for long or concentrated on one place except when she was putting on her eye shadow. She'd learned to apply lipstick without a mirror years ago. Jason nagged her about the fifteen pounds she'd gained after the kids were born, but she'd never been able to lose them. For encouragement, she replayed her sister Lisa's warning that if she lost weight she'd collapse into a bunch of wrinkles, just like her neighbors.

The thought of her sister filled her with pleasure. They talked regularly on Sunday mornings. As her friends had drifted slowly out of her life, Lisa had become even more important. The loss of her friends had been one of the more unexpected parts of her mourning. She had decided she reminded them of their own fragile hold on normalcy. If it could happen to her, why not them? She still missed them, one in particular.

*****

Anna had been her best friend since her marriage. Her husband worked with Jason. They went to church together, their children played together. Dylan and Timothy, Anna's son, had just started T-ball that summer and would be making their first communion together in the spring. When Maureen started to question her faith, it had been too much for Anna. She had started calling instead of coming by, then the calls stopped. When Maureen called, Anna was always on her way out the door. She hadn't seen Anna again until two years later. They'd nearly collided in the aisle of the drugstore, and Anna had almost tipped her cart over in an effort to turn the corner and pretend she hadn't seen Maureen. Timothy had been with her, and Maureen's heart contracted at how much he'd grown. She wondered what Dylan would have looked like at the age of seven, going on eight. When Anna saw her look she reached out a hand, then pulled it back as if she'd burnt herself. Maureen could see her mentally determining that she could not risk talking to her. She still had Timothy. Maureen had taken the fall for all of them. Bryan had put his small hand on her cheek, looking up into her eyes as her friend nodded like an old acquaintance and turned into the next aisle. She had added Anna to her losses.

*****

She fluffed her hair one last time, and headed downstairs. On the counter she saw a plate smeared with red sauce, a note sticking out from under it:

Don't wait up—you know these meetings always take longer than they're supposed to. J

She stared at the wall calendar, the note drooping from her hand. First Thursday of the month—Toastmaster's Club. She'd never really understood what he did there. She was sure she'd asked at one time, but Bryan's basketball games had been on Thursdays and she was team mother. How easily she and Jason had drifted into parallel lives. The fresh bread sat on the counter, hacked off at the end. He must have just soaked the sauce up with it while he watched the sports news on cable. Maureen heard the sigh that escaped her. God, she was turning into her mother. Long suffering wife, a role she had sworn she would never adopt. She turned away from the calendar. She shouldn't have tried to surprise him. He probably hadn't noticed the set table. If he had, he would have skipped the meeting just this once. Or was she, once again, making excuses for a man she could only love by creating him? That note ... so cold, so impersonal. She put a pot of water on to boil fettuccine for one.

In the dining room, she lit a candle and watched as light spread over the cloth and pooled at the end of the table, exposing a red circle splashed on the crisp linen. Her heart hesitated, then she cried out in protest. Bread crumbs lay scattered on the crumpled napkin next to a used wine glass. She moved the candles and wine off the tablecloth and took it into the kitchen, soaking the stained area with baking soda and cold water. She left it in the sink and went back into the dining room. She got the other candle lit on the third try, and sat down in her chair. "Jason," she cried out from the raw anguish of her heart. "Who are you?"

The blood on her skirt, the stained cloth, Dylan lying on the pool deck, a perfect red halo forming around his head as the towel absorbed his blood.

She poured herself a glass of wine and drank it down. Later, the wine bottle empty, the candles gutted out, she caught a whiff of smoke. In the kitchen she found the water boiled dry, the pot starting to bulge on the bottom. She had enough sense left to pull it off the burner before she went upstairs. She crawled into Jason's side of the bed, snuggling into the valley created there by his body. She remembered how she used to lie against his back, knees in the bend of his knees, her head in the curve of his shoulder. She was almost as tall as Jason, and they had been a good fit until her pregnancy with Dylan. Then she had started sleeping on her own side of the bed, her back against his, arms crossed over her stomach. Shortly after Dylan died, they had bought a king-sized bed to keep from disturbing each other. The dents in the mattress were like two carved wooden bows curving away from each other. She inhaled the faint scent of woody aftershave on Jason's pillow and fell asleep.

Chapter Two

Morning sun probed the window and slivered behind Maureen's eyes. She struggled up blindly, felt for the edge of the bed, finding only the smoothness of the cotton comforter. Last night hung around her like a gray cloud. Whistling floated up the stairs, the door slammed, and the throaty sound of the Lexus faded down the street. She couldn't describe the pain in her head. It didn't seem possible that her father could have felt like this every morning and continued to drink. Eyes shut, Maureen slowly drew her legs over the side. Maybe this was the purpose of drinking—it took every ounce of concentration you had. She inched her way to the bathroom, eyes still closed, feeling her way along the wall carefully, her wounded hand aching. An insect-like sensitivity invaded her fingers. She felt every hairline crack in the super gloss champagne beige paint. It was how she managed to function after Dylan died, this elaborate attention to detail. Her throbbing hand slipped on the wall. Careful, she told herself. Slow and careful.

For nearly seventeen years, every minute of frantic activity had built the dam that blocked the flow of memory. PTA president, volunteer for the Heart Association, Diabetes Foundation, the blind, the lame, the homeless, the players of soccer, basketball, and baseball, swimmers and Girl Scouts, Boy Scouts, tutor at the elementary school, band mother, entertainer of the year for Jason's business associates, gourmet cook ... thinking of it, she swayed where she stood, keeping her hand on the wall. Like a beaver, she had worked patiently, mending each breach that threatened her home, her family, her sanity. Now she could feel the water rushing in.

Images flickered in her mind like the home movies her dad had shown on a sheet taped to the living room wall. Her bloody skirt. The red splash on the table cloth. The bloody towel under Dylan's head. Her system required vigilance. She slid to the bathroom floor, her legs unable to hold her, her sweaty palms sliding down the wall. She surrendered to the movie.

*****

She watched herself walk toward Dylan, his lovely, round, six-year-old face turned upwards with the innocent expectation of a puppy. There was no fear. He trusted everyone and was in love with his first grade teacher. He had probably been running through the backyard after the school bus dropped him off. This was the part she filled in like an altered tape.

Maureen had been bathing Gabi while she waited for the babysitter. Tonight was her exam, the last class she would be able to take in her Master's program before the baby was born. She noted the time and wondered why the bus Dylan rode home from school on Tuesdays was late. No shiver of wind passed over her. No dark clouds covered the sun. The air was alive with birdsong and the smell of orange blossoms.

The paramedics said it looked like he had skidded on the wet deck and hit his head on the way into the water. They'd arrived shortly after Maureen pulled him from the water to the deck, wrapping him in a white towel, after the bus driver confirmed he had indeed ridden home to Martinique Drive at three o'clock. He still wore the apple badge that stated he was Dodd School's Helper of the Week. The red and green construction paper apple, assembled by the young Mrs. Harper, had bled into his white shirt. He had looked so much older with his brown curls slicked wet to his head. A bruise on his temple showed blue as the deepest part of the sea, just above the wound that ran down over his ear. She tried desperately to breathe life into him, willing his lungs to take the breath from her lungs. The leafless elms of a Florida January drooped over the fence, more appropriate that day than the feverishly blooming bougainvillea scattering wet blossoms around the pool. Maureen saw scarlet petals smeared on the bottom of Dylan's new sneakers when the paramedics took him from her and carried him to the ambulance. A car passed down the street, music pouring from its windows. She had been stunned by the sound as she climbed in the back of the ambulance next to her dead child, pool water dripping from her hair. The medic wrapped her in a blanket and she lifted Dylan to her, rubbing his cold hands with hers. At the hospital, they'd finally given her a shot before they could uncurl her hands from him. She would see forever his sneakered foot dangling over the arm of the nurse as the door at the end of the hallway closed and her world turned dark.

She had listened to the explanations of Father Dolan with a carefully arranged attention. Her mother and Sister Angela, Dylan's First Communion counselor, talked about Maureen's own little angel who had the ear of the Blessed Mother. Personally, she believed the dead hovered a little closer to earth. The thought had flickered and died because she had known that if she tried to sense Dylan nearby, she would have to agree that he was dead. Then she would begin to scream, and they would give her shots to stop the screaming, and Gabi would be afraid, and she would harm the baby that grew inside her, the one with only a month to go before he entered the world.

Dylan was buried on a perfect Florida winter day. The air hummed with color and life, white clouds piled like whipped cream. The hole in the ground was protected from their eyes by a garish carpet shamed by the real grass around it. The mourners left while the casket still stood high on its bier, surrounded by carnations in wicker baskets. But Maureen knew. She sensed the machinery lurking under the simulated St. Augustine grass that was ready to lower Dylan into the ground, cover him with real dirt, leave him forever away from her. She stumbled as Jason led her to the car, her dry eyes looking down on an ant hill writhing with activity, already repairing the damage her foot had done.

That night, four pound six ounce Bryan was born, work she performed quietly, tears flowing into her hair, pooling in the hollows of her neck and shoulders. She didn't make a sound during her labor. She saw Jason holding her hand, his eyes blank with fear, but she couldn't feel him. She had been as alone as an old woman set adrift on an ice floe. When they brought Bryan to her, her breasts ached but produced no milk. Lisa had fed him from a tiny bottle. Her sister stayed for two weeks, sitting with her at night, talking quietly and steadily to keep her sane. Mrs. Quinn stayed at the house with Gabi, who, at two, couldn't understand where her brother Dylan and her mommy had gone. No one had known how to tell her.

*****

Under the roar of a pounding surf, she could hear Jason asking Doctor Johnson from down the street about the wine she drank. They stood over the bed, discussing her as if she wasn't there.

"Well, it didn't help," he said, "but it probably didn't hurt either. Just make sure she stays in bed for a couple of days. These viral things usually pass pretty quickly. Make sure she gets plenty of fluids …" His voice trailed off as Jason walked him downstairs. Maureen remembered that Dr. Johnson was a retired optometrist. She guessed a doctor was a doctor and stayed in bed with relief. At least she knew why she had weakened and what she would be doing for the next two or three days. Her inactivity had a purpose—an invisible virus that needed the run of her body for a while. She slept through the weekend, waking for periodic bowls of soup and iced drinks Jason brought, his usually distracted look replaced by one of concern and something else. Something that looked like the old fear. Monday, he brought her tea and toast in the morning along with an ice bucket full of soft drinks to last until he came home from the office. She started reading *Like Water for Chocolate*. The heroine's mind continually created new realities. It seemed to fit her mood. She had a hard time returning to the real world when Jason came in from work. He heated soup for her, and as she ate, he talked. He sounded like a hospital visitor with a nurse in the room, describing the heat, how his new partner was working out. He continued to sleep in Bryan's room as he had the night she'd finished the bottle of Burgundy, and she continued to refuse to let him phone her mother.

On Wednesday morning, after Jason left for work, she slid shakily into warm water in the claw-footed tub she'd rescued from her mother's old house. She looked at her wavering feet, the chipped polish on her toenails, the calluses on her heels. Inside her head, she heard a gusting sigh, then her mother's voice: "Maureen, will you *ever* learn to be a lady? It takes so little you know. Grooming. Carriage. Nothing drastic."

Maureen closed her eyes and sank deeper into the water. When her father died, her mother had moved to Naples, Florida, and reinvented herself. Gone was the natural gray hair, the cotton shirtwaists, even the Midwestern accent. On the phone, she became a sort of New England Bette Davis. She had silver hair waved tight to her head like a twenties movie star, wore short-jacketed suits with gold buttons and subtle braid trim and carried little boxy purses with chains instead of straps. Eleanor Quinn's perfume was quiet and expensive, as were her escorts. Her grandchildren were instructed to call her Eleanor.

The voice whispered around the tile. "Maureen, there are certain things a man wants in a woman, at least a man of stature, like Jason. You need to pay more attention to yourself."

Maureen sank to her chin in the water, remembering the conversation with her mother before her latest trip. It had been eerily similar to those they'd had since she was twelve years old, long before Jason came along.

She opened her eyes and studied her wavering reflection in the wet tile. *Your mother's right. You will never be a lady,* she scolded her blurred image. Not that she hadn't tried, and she'd been quite successful in the areas the public saw. But in private, she still had chipped polish and calluses, preferred caftans and bare feet to Laura Ashley or even Calvin Klein, and she still brought home stray dogs and needy people, just as she had as a child.

*****

At twelve, she'd been awkward, puppy-footed, freckled and tall for her age. She had hunched her shoulders inward to bring herself down to size and cover the offending changes in her body.

Her sister, Lisa, two years older, had been athletic and surefooted. Lisa's black hair was smooth as river mud, a gift from the French side of their mother's family. Maureen was all Gaelic, her dark red hair electric frizz in the humidity of summer in Illinois. Maureen looked like her father used to before the "sickness" got him, a euphemism her grandmother had used for the many men in the family who drank. In Antoinette's Charm School, Maureen had struggled to balance volume eight of the Encyclopedia Britannica on her head. She got up to seven steps one wintry day and the class applauded. She was good at the paper work and could tell you the proper form of address for kings and dukes, but Antoinette had given her mother her money back.

Through ballet and acrobatics, she continued to disappoint her parents, but she knew a secret, one she didn't tell anyone. She was a singer, and when the time came, she would sing like Judy Garland and everyone would remember her. Someone would say, "I always knew there was something about that girl," and another would respond, "If you had asked me, I could have told you." In the meantime, she sang in the church choir at Blessed Mother of the Angels and kept her voice properly modulated for the alto section. She was head alto because she could read music, thanks to eight years of piano lessons. When she thought Hilda Morgan was sliding off F sharp, she would nudge her and hum the note into her ear. The air smelled like cheese when the hum wafted back out.

*****

Maureen dunked her feet and let the flat soap bubbles cover her imperfect toes. She envied that girl who had been so sure of her talent, hoarding her secret dream. Maureen had no idea where she'd gone. When she started her Master's, she resigned herself to teaching music to those who could still share their talent with the world. Hers had gone. She slapped the bubbles, then pulled the drain chain with her toe, sending the tepid water whooshing down the pipe.

The sound echoed back to the day she had stood beside the pool watching a contractor drain the water before breaking up the concrete. She had become a single, feeling organism, going with the water in a torrent out to the sea. She wouldn't have to think or feel anymore, just go, wet and slithery, an eel passing through the small drain where Dylan's essence was disappearing. The sun had gone behind a cloud as the dark water whirled around the bottom of the algae-covered pool. The older of the two workmen, compassion lighting his sun-weathered face, had gently taken her arm and led her inside.

*****

She stood in the tub. That wasn't her anymore. It was another life. The virus had really affected her brain. She rinsed off in the warm water of the shower. She slathered lotion down her neck, over her round shoulders, the soft skin of her wet breasts. She smoothed almond scented cream on her legs while she was still wet, something the lady at the beauty counter swore would keep her skin moist and youthful. She wrapped up in one of her favorite thick white towels and stepped out of the tub. A powerful weakness attacked her calves and knees. Her heart skipped, and she leaned against the clammy wall of the bathroom under the open window. The school bus stopped next door, releasing faint voices, like the piping of small sea birds calling. One lone child cried, and Maureen felt the pull, that flowing out to encompass, to smooth, to make right all that was uneven or unfair. What had she thought? That when her children walked out the door it just dried up? Maybe not, but she hadn't expected this strong surge. She wondered if she had the strength to divert it. And to where? She couldn't fathom the idea of all that energy directed inward toward herself. It wasn't possible. She struggled into her bedroom and felt blindly for the edge of the bed, knocking over a stack of books she had been dipping into before the kids left for school. Most of them were about the search for meaning or the latest on menopause. Without the anchor of her Catholicism, Maureen had been drifting through what she privately thought of as her "belief of the week." The last course she audited at the junior college had been Eastern Philosophy, but recently, she'd discovered writers who spoke more directly to her questions. She'd cleaned out the library on the subject of spirituality and women. She picked up the books and stacked them neatly on the table. On the top, a book called *The Song of Eve,* by Manuela Dunn Mascetti, featured a painting of a red-haired Eve holding an apple and looking very pleased with herself. Maureen was half finished with that book and found the archetypal stories strangely disturbing, particularly the story of Demeter. She would have to return these books. Surely by now they were long overdue. She crawled under the covers. The air-conditioning must be down to sixty degrees. She was so cold.

She slept until noon, rousing herself to open a can of soup and heat it in the microwave. She couldn't continue like this, keeping Dylan at bay by sleeping, refusing to move on with her life. She was getting weaker every day. She had to talk to Jason. She sat straighter in the chair, practicing the words she would use to ask her husband of twenty-four years how it was possible that they had never talked about Dylan. Their child's name stands like a wall between them. This time she will not let him turn away. This time she won't ask him in bed where he can roll over and place the pillows between them. She won't ask him in the den where he can turn on the television and cover her words. She will ask him when he comes in from work. She will ask him why they are strangers in parallel worlds, never diverging, never touching. She will ask him how it is possible that they are still together.

At eight o'clock, she was in the living room in her robe, a cup of herbal tea in her hand. Jason came in through the kitchen and opened the refrigerator, where a salad waited for their dinner. He opened a bottle of beer, and she heard the cap rolling in the empty wastebasket.

"I'm in the living room, Jason," she called. "Bring your beer in here."

She heard him inhale. He knew. Several long minutes later, he stood in the door, his expression guarded.

"You're up. I'm glad, but you didn't have to fix dinner."

An area at the center of her ached at the sight of his thin face veiled in dread.

"Jason, I'm not sick ..." She stopped, seeing his look of disbelief as he took in her bathrobe, her shaking hands.

"What I mean is, physically, I'm not." She took a deep breath. "Please. Sit down. We need to talk."

He stayed in the doorway.

"Please, Jason. This is hard enough."

"If you're going to tell me you're leaving," he said through stiff lips, the beer glass clenched in his hands, "I'd rather stand."

"Leaving?" Her brain reeled. She couldn't think of what to say.

"I thought this would happen when the kids left. I can't say I'm surprised."

"I'm not leaving, Jason." She closed her eyes against the glow of his relief. He left the door and sat in the chair across from hers, only the table, the lamp and the wall they'd built, between them.

"Maybe we could start with why you thought I'd leave," Maureen said, sensing an opening. She watched as his lawyer's mind picked out and discarded pieces of information, argument, summations.

"We've been on separate tracks for years. I just figured you were here for the kids ..." He shrugged. "I guess that's it."

"That's why I wanted to talk to you. We *have* been in what Bryan would call 'parallel universes,' and it's been since Dylan died." She waited as the words echoed around the room like loud voices in a church. She'd said it, finally, out loud. She waited.

"Why do you want to bring this up now? We managed to get on with our lives. The kids are doing fine."

"But *we're* not doing fine. You admitted as much yourself." She settled back in the chair, trying to think clearly, not get him riled up. She could feel the tension radiating from him like wires plugged into her warning signals.

"You're just at loose ends, that's all. Your mom called it 'empty nest.'"

"You talked to my mother? Jason, you promised." She struggled to lower her voice.

"She called, dammit. What was I supposed to do? Lie to her? Anyway, she's not coming. I told her you were better and that we could work it out for ourselves."

"Will we? We quit being partners so long ago. I don't know you. I don't know how you feel or what you think about things."

"What things? Maureen, everybody isn't like you. Some of us just go about our lives. We don't have time to analyze everything to death, and we probably wouldn't if we had the time."

She felt the logic of his words hit her mind. Maybe it *was* her. Maybe Jason had dealt with Dylan while she was walling him up. Or maybe his way of being busy—work, golf, Toastmasters, various business committees—wasn't all that different from what she'd done except he could keep right on doing it. His life wasn't going to change with the kids gone.

Jason's voice woke her from her reverie. "Maureen? Maybe you should think about taking a trip. Lisa is always after you to come to California. Now that the kids are gone, you can do anything you want."

She nodded as his words echoed her thoughts. She was still too weak for this conversation. He didn't have the television or the pillows between them, but she felt a barrier even stronger. The barrier of his mind. She needed to work on this alone. Maybe when she was completely well. Maybe then they could talk. An enormous wave of heat rolled up her chest, into her neck and face. Even her ears were hot. She knew she would leave her outline on the chair when she stood.

"You're right, Jason," she managed. "Why don't you go ahead and have dinner? I think I overdid it a little for the first day. I'll just go on up to bed."

His relief was palpable. "Let me help you." He put his arm around her back. Her robe was soaking wet.

"It feels like your fever broke," he said. "That's a good sign. Be sure you change to something dry before you get in bed." He helped her up the stairs and into their bedroom. Moments later she heard the cabinets open and close as he served himself dinner.

Chapter Three

The next morning Jason was gone when she got up at seven. She sat cross-legged on the carpet in the bedroom and attempted to meditate for the first time in a week. Yoga and meditation classes had been her salvation. Every morning she visualized a cool room surrounding a low glass table with a vase of tall, glorious, purple iris. There was no roof, since her imagination allowed perfect weather. Sometimes it was day, sometimes a starry night, but in this place she was able to calm herself and begin her day. This morning the room was out of focus and she had trouble seeing the flowers. After several minutes, she gave up. She'd probably had enough sitting still for a while. She dressed and went downstairs, determined to reclaim the details of her life. She whipped through the house, pushing the vacuum cleaner back and forth over the living room rug that bore only her own footprints.

At eleven o'clock, the mail arrived. Exhausted, she fixed a glass of iced tea and went outside. She sat on the patio swing and sorted through the mail. Sunlight pierced the leaves of the oak and sprinkled over her, the heat already wilting the zinnias in their clay pots.

She dozed in the sun, saw herself going to school wearing the clothes she'd worn in the '60s, but her face and figure were those of an eighty-year-old woman. Everyone else was a teenager. She woke in a sweat, her body superheated from another hot flash. She'd been having them off and on for the past six months. Anger flared in her at the inadequacies of descriptions such as "hot flashes." No words described the feeling of having your entire body consumed in flames, then chilled and drenched in sweat. Her mother said she'd been fifty when hers began, suggesting that Maureen's body was responsible for her early menopausal symptoms. Maureen had been reading up on this and could find nothing that supported her mother's opinion. She was, however, interested in the sound of the word. The pause part seemed to her to be particularly encouraging, though some of the women in the PTA and at the club had whispered "menopause" as if it were the end, not the middle, of something.

Two squirrels argued in the sprawling oak surrounded by azalea bushes. The bushes were homely right now, without their spring blossoms. They had been flush with pink when she planted them there, where the pool had been. Azaleas were not her favorites, but the house on Martinique was brick Tudor, more Atlanta than Tampa. The neighborhood had brick streets that the city periodically threatened to pave. Huge oaks shaded the landscaped houses, belying the major city lying just blocks away, and her azaleas thrived.

She wondered, not for the first time, if she was having a mental breakdown. She couldn't concentrate on anything for more than a few seconds. She closed her eyes, imagining her thoughts emptying like water from a pitcher, but again, her meditation technique didn't work. Sweat puddled in the small of her back. Rubbing her stiff neck, she got up from the swing and went into the kitchen. The big wall clock ticked firmly, its hands joined at twelve. The bills waited, and the meat she intended for dinner was still in the freezer. She glanced at the calendar. Sweet relief. Thursday again and another meeting for Jason—a lawyers' committee of some kind. She didn't have to think about dinner. She sat at her desk, fixing her mind firmly on one task.

Mid-afternoon Maureen put a thick rubber band around the stack of stamped bills and set them on the hall table. She rubbed her back with one hand and looked over the mail she'd set aside. A creamy white envelope felt thick and important. She turned it over. Mr. and Mrs. Wilson Judson, with an Avila address. Ugh. Probably another one of Jason's clients requiring a trip to Morgan's Jewelry and Fine Gifts for the obligatory crystal bowl.

"Listen to yourself," she said aloud. "Such a martyr. Tired after a half day of routine housework." She heard her mother in her own voice.

She slid the wedding invitation from the envelope, leaning over her calendar to note the date. The floor tilted and heat radiated from her center to the roots of her hair … desert heat sucking her dry, turning her body into a furnace so hot her reading glasses fogged over. Damn. She fought for control, her shoulders and neck tense, her fingers gripping the pen. A door at the end of a dark tunnel floated closer. She closed her eyes, breathing in and out steadily, stroking the smooth vellum of the announcement in her hand. She willed herself to wipe out the tunnel, replace it with that cool white room with irises on the table and the roof open to the stars. Slowly, the heat receded and she could see the purple flowers. Something else, something she had never wanted to see, was on the table. It was a stationery box spilling over with cards and large white envelopes. Where had that come from? She didn't want to see that. No. She wouldn't see that. She skittered off, but her mind came back to it, insistent. She saw her hand reach for one of the cards. Its large black funereal letters vibrated in front of her. *Sympathy in Your Loss*, it said. She touched it, and it fell to the floor. One in particular she knew wasn't there, the one that said *We Know How You Feel*. That one she had torn to shreds. Another lay on the table: *Be Joyful for He Is With the Lord*. She remembered trying to understand the word joy, feel it in her mouth, a real word. But it read like Latin, like her Missal in Catholic school in eighth grade when she'd first felt her faith slipping.

The box was stored on a shelf at the back of the linen closet. Her deep breaths turned shallow and ragged. She pushed up from the chair and moved stiffly up the carpeted stairs. All those years since she had tied the box with a ribbon, stored it high on the shelf and deep in her unconscious. Why today? Her legs shook. She dropped to her knees, crawling up the stairs, a supplicant on the Via Dolorosa.

She saw herself crouching in the back corner of that same closet a year after Dylan's death. She had awakened that morning and known that she couldn't recall his voice. How could that be? Since they were babies, with her eyes closed, she could tell which one of her children's blankets she held for the laundry. Their smells were as specific to her as roses or peaches. For weeks after, whenever Gabi and Bryan were down for their naps, she sat in that closet with her nose buried in Dylan's blanket breathing his scent, straining to remember his voice.

*****

It had been a sultry morning when she'd come home from taking Gabi to the doctor and found her mother in the laundry room washing Dylan's clothes. Her mother had looked her in the eye, determination on her face.

"Jason agrees with me, dear." She'd put a hand out toward Maureen who stood pilloried in the door with feverish Gabi whimpering in her arms.

"Maureen, don't look at me like that. It's for your own recovery. Keeping that basket of unwashed clothes … it just isn't healthy." She withdrew her hand nervously. "I didn't go looking, you know," she said, drawing herself up. "I put Bryan down for his nap and went into the closet to get a light weight blanket—you know the one on his bed is winter weight."

She stopped, fluttering her hands together like moth wings. "Oh Maureen, what could you be thinking of? You have these babies to care for …"

Maureen had fled out the kitchen door and up the stairs, her mother's pleading following behind her. She had taken Gabi's shoes and socks off and laid her gently on her bed, pulling the sheet up to her damp little neck, stroking her face until she slept. She had walked down the hallway toward the open closet door, her legs weighted, willing Dylan's blanket to be there, the one he'd slept with even when he was too big to carry it in front of his friends. The yellow ducks on its border had faded to beige and the blue field was grey, but he had tucked it under his shoulder and lain his head on it every night, a ritual that had replaced sucking his thumb when he'd started kindergarten. Sometimes, in the early pearl gray mornings when she went to wake him for school, she would find him with a damp corner of the blanket in his slightly open mouth.

That day, she had been on her hands and knees, searching, when her mother came up the stairs with the carefully washed and folded clothes.

On top of the pile was a precise row of clean, starched, marching ducks. Her mother had touched Maureen's hair, concern tight on her face.

"I didn't get rid of them, dear, though Jason felt I should. I just washed them, that's all. No harm done." And she had laid the clothes in Maureen's arms.

The smell of bleach had burned her nose when she lifted the blanket to her face, and Maureen had put Dylan in another walled up room in the house of her spirit.

*****

Now that room was cracking open along with everything else, like adobe surrendering slowly to flood waters. She opened the closet door and stood on tiptoe, feeling her way to the back of the shelf. What if Jason had thrown the box away? What did she want anyway? She felt driven, all logic and control trickling through the fissures, seeping away. With all that ballast gone, she was liable to float away over the house like a helium balloon, a little speck by the time she reached the Gulf of Mexico. Her fingers grazed a slick surface under the woolen scarves they'd used in Illinois when they had visited her folks at Christmas. She slid the box toward her, like a priest bringing the chalice out of the curtains inside the tabernacle. Her chest tightened, and she struggled to breathe as the bright silk that had lived in darkness nearly seventeen years came into the light. She clutched the box and settled slowly to the floor, carefully slipping the yellowing satin ribbon off the corners. Her ears were ringing—probably the telephone far off in the empty house. She took a deep breath and lifted the lid.

On top was the Mass card from Dylan's funeral, a seated Jesus surrounded by children. Her eyes saw each letter in three dimensions:

DYLAN JASON MANLEY
BORN: NOVEMBER 24, 1967
DIED: JANUARY 17, 1974
SUFFER THE LITTLE CHILDREN TO COME UNTO ME

Under the card, a dried white rose from the spray on the casket lay intact, its tiny leaves brown and crisp.

*****

Like an icon, she saw Dylan emblazoned on her mind. His face had glowed inside the white satin coffin liner, makeup masking the gash in his forehead so it looked like a thin pencil mark down to his left ear, the bruise mauve in the candlelight. It had been the night of the Rosary, and she remembered looking at Dylan and feeling detached, wondering where he really was. This copy of her child, like a 3-D picture, was a trick. She saw herself standing beside herself, watched herself touching his hair, saw herself noticing that it was stiff and slightly green from the chlorine in the pool. When Jason knelt to pray, she had stayed still, except for her hands stroking her stomach, wondering how and what she was supposed to feel. The baby in her belly had been quiet for a change, gathering strength for the ordeal ahead, and she had clasped her hands together across that life and held on.

*****

She unclenched her hands and forced her mind back to the box. She opened and reread letters she didn't remember seeing before, from friends who were long gone from her life. She was surprised that she had ever known some of them. She turned the newspaper obituary notices upside down, and there at the bottom of the box she found a card, unopened, from Stephen. Stephen, her first love. She didn't remember getting the card or why she had put it there unread. Lisa and her mother had taken care of the cards after she had torn the first one to pieces. Still, she remembered signing all the thank you notes. She opened the envelope. It was a blank card with a note written in that script as familiar to her as her own:

"I feel your pain and pray for your healing. If you need me, anytime, remember, I am always with you—like the stars."

It was signed "Stephen" and included an address and telephone number in Oregon. She put the card back into the envelope, memory pouring through the cracks, making a lake of her mind. She trembled violently at the thought of what else might surface, wondering how Stephen had known about Dylan. How had he kept track of her over the years, and she had never known where he was? Why? She leaned back against the closet door and closed her eyes. She was so tired. Stephen stood like a shadow in her mind's eye. He was an artist, but he had joined the Navy instead of accepting a scholarship to Northwestern University. She had begged him to go to art school, but he'd said he needed to make money to help his divorced mother and younger brother. He said he would go later. She wondered for the thousandth time what had happened to him. She rubbed her temples, letting the card slip into her lap. Another hot flash came and subsided, taking her to late summer in Illinois, the first time she met Stephen.

*****

She had finished her freshman year in high school and taken a job detasseling corn, not the job her father had for her in his office. The truck picked her up at the end of her gravel road at four o'clock in the morning. She remembered that the chill wet had soaked through her triple layered clothes by the time she worked her way down the first row of corn in the half-light. By six o'clock, the sun was glinting off the dew on the razor sharp leaf edges. She had thin slices in her wrists just above the too short gloves, and drops of blood pricked out, then flowed together like rain drops on a window. By the eleven o'clock lunch break, she had stripped down to one layer of clothes. Like apparitions from purgatory, steam rose over the dark green stalks as the workers converged on the flatbed truck. She and Stephen had come together at the edge of the field, and when he lifted her wrist to look at the blood, they made one large column of vapor rising into the hard blue August sky.

When her father found out about Stephen, he had forbidden even telephone calls. She was fifteen and not allowed to date. Stephen was eighteen.

He had been pulled out of school frequently to work in the fields and was entering his senior year. She waited impatiently for school to start. In the fall, they shared lunches under the trees, talks at basketball games. They wrote letters, and he included pictures he had drawn. She still had them in her high school scrap book. He had invited her to his senior prom, but her father said no, so he didn't go either. At his graduation, Maureen had sung with the girl's ensemble, every note of the benediction aimed straight at him.

The last time she saw Stephen was an August day one year later, just before he left for Naval duty in Key West. She was working at the State Fair in Springfield, and he came to meet her after she finished her shift at the 4-H lemonade stand. She was squeezing the last of the lemons, her hands coated with the dribbling lemon-sugar mixture, her clothes soaked from humidity, when she saw Stephen coming through the crowd. He stood out because he lacked a cowboy hat, an FFA hat, or a cap advertising some tractor company. His brown hair curled below his ears, and she had felt a tender grief at the thought of his induction haircut. He saw her finishing up and waved, his smile arching through the air. She savored the sight of his profile, the thin nose and high cheekbones earned from his Cheyenne grandmother. He set his back against a nearby building to watch the flow of people and the lights blooming one by one on the midway. She even loved the way his well-worn boot propped against the wall, holding the weight of his rangy body slightly bent toward the ground. Maureen envied his ease. He was at home in his skin as she was not. He looked into her and said it was good, like God when he'd created the earth. When she was with him, she felt it was true, felt ripe like Eve in the garden. She rinsed away the sugar from between her fingers, tossed her apron in the heap behind the counter and hurried toward him.

The smell of the cornfields stirred in the evening breeze, scented with Lake Springfield, cotton candy and the warm bodies of cows settling down in the barns. She was acutely aware of the skin on her upper arm and thigh where they brushed against his cotton shirt and jeans. She was sure that if she looked, she would see little sparks like baby fireflies striking each time they took a step. She memorized the look of the midway as the sunset out on the plains softened it to old rose. Even the barkers at the tents of circus freaks modulated their voices, singing, "She walks, she talks, she crawls on her belly like a reptile," as if it were the Agnus Dei at nine o'clock Mass. They waited, hand-in-hand, in front of the double ferris wheel, watching it slowly change from upright to horizontal like the clock of the world. She was one with all of it, her spirit rising and falling with the couples whose faint voices fell from the top like cherry blossoms floating to the ground.

A swing descended in front of them, and after they stepped into it, Stephen carefully shut the bar in front of her. Slowly, the majestic circles lifted high above the fairgrounds. Warm air dried the sweat on her skin and lifted her cotton skirt like a lily. The dome of the Capitol and Lincoln's tomb glowed under the mauve and orange sky. At the edge of the earth, pinpricks of stars were poised, waiting their turn. Stephen's arm tightened around her, and when he leaned to kiss her, the swing tilted back. Her stomach dropped as the huge gears swung their wheel up and over the other one, but she wasn't afraid. She would stay aloft as long as he held her, no matter where the wheel went. As they descended, she memorized the generous contours of his mouth as he told her that they were forever like the stars. He put his senior ring on a chain around her neck.

When he left the next day, Maureen was still a virgin, and she had not yet taken the course that would tell her that a star's light had usually gone out by the time it reached her eyes. He had promised to come back for her, and she waited. Waited to be of age, waited to be rescued, waited for life to begin. His first letter included a picture of him in his Navy uniform, his hair shorn. She had put that picture in the bottom of her keepsake box. They wrote for a year and a half, and then came the last letter when he told her she needed to find someone else because she wanted children, and he didn't want to be a father. She realized then that it was only in her letters to him that there was talk of home and family, children together. His letters were only about the two of them. He told her he was being transferred overseas and this was goodbye. She was sure that if she ever got time alone with him she could convince him of the rightness of them. She never got the chance. Her letters came back "Address Unknown." It was as if he was swallowed whole like Jonah and carried down to the bottom of the sea.

She went to see his mother, but she was far gone in alcoholism and couldn't tell Maureen anything. She found out later that Stephen's father had died of liver disease. That was when it began to make sense. Of course he was afraid to have children. She replayed in her mind her side of their conversations, her letters to him. Always she had talked of her children, their children. She had told him about her father, how he treated her when he drank. She yearned to have a family of her own. Somehow, in her mind, it would make up for her dad. She would be a good mother, teaching her children love instead of fear. Through all of this, Stephen had never mentioned his mother and dad having the same addiction as her father. In school, they had studied the genetic structure of plants, and he had talked about the things he saw in cattle, the flaws passed down generation after generation. Of course he would choose not to have children, especially with her.

In her despair, Maureen had decided to join the Peace Corps, but by graduation in 1962, the University of Florida had offered her a music scholarship. Florida was far enough away that she would have an excuse for not going home on holidays, the times that triggered the worst of her father's drinking, so she went.

In Florida, Maureen walled Stephen up in a corner of her mind. That corner had a secret door, and she let him out every once in a while over the years and asked him what would have become of them. Would they have been kind to each other? Once, more alone than she had thought possible, she called him into her mind, asked him what he would have done if their son had died. Would he have held her, rocked her, let his tears join with hers until they created a river? In the silence there was no answer. Dylan wouldn't have come from Stephen. She had sealed him back into his corner and applied fresh mortar to the seams in the wall. Until today, he had stayed there.

*****

The memory was so sharp, she shook her head, surprised not to feel a pony tail brushing against her neck. She put almost everything back in the box, laying it in the bottom drawer of her dresser, under her sweaters. The note from Stephen she slid into her apron pocket. As she stood in the bedroom door, the phone rang again. She let the answering machine pick up and heard her mother's voice hanging in the air:

"Oh dear, sorry to have missed you again ... will call when the ship docks in Nassau ... hope you're fine. Didn't the kids leave for school this week? You should have lots of time now to do what you want. Off to cocktails darling ... see you next month."

Maureen stood still as the echoes of her mother's breathless message eased into the corners of the house. She could picture years going by this way, see herself leaning in the doorway for two days, sipping coffee on the patio, another day, hearing people's voices flow around her like currents. Before she knew it, her fifties would be here and gone and then ... She curled her fingers around the envelope in her pocket. She heard her mother's words: "... lots of time now to do what you want." And then there was Jason, telling her she should go visit Lisa. In all these years she'd never traveled alone. The family went to the beach every summer for two weeks, and when Gabi had graduated from high school, she and Maureen had gone to Atlanta. There had been the one year when Jason earned his first bonus and they went to Key West. That was the extent of her travel.

Lisa had asked her to come to San Francisco year after year, and always, she'd had an excuse. Why? What was keeping her here? And San Francisco wasn't that far from Oregon, was it? She stopped herself. What did that have to do with anything? The envelope crackled in her hand. Sixteen plus years. People didn't stay in one place that long. But she had. And he knew that. How? Did he know she was still here, still wrapped in her shroud of mourning? She shook herself. Melodrama. That's what this was. Her mother had called her Greta Garbo. Obviously there was a reason.

Maureen went back into her bedroom, took a deep breath, then picked up the phone. Someone else had taken over her body, was dialing the number in Stephen's note. On the fourth ring, there was a chime, then the deep sweet sound of a woman's voice:

"You have reached Emania Lodge. Stephen and Brigit are unavailable right now, but we would like to return your call. Please leave your name and number and we'll return to you as soon as we can. If you're calling about the Woman's Rites on Labor Day weekend, please press one for more information."

There was a chime, and without thinking, Maureen pressed the button.

"This is Brigit. On Labor Day weekend, we will be holding a workshop exclusively for women who are entering or experiencing the fullness of their moon, otherwise known as menopause. Rituals from ancient cultures will be used to celebrate this most sacred and wonderful of women's times. If you would like to join us, please leave a message including your name, address, and telephone number and I will contact you."

She hung up. She stared at her hand on the phone as if it belonged to a stranger. A vague excitement grew in her belly like the stirring of a small animal. That there should be something to celebrate about this experience of menopause was a new point of view, but even more exciting was the idea of going, of seeing what had become of Stephen. She didn't believe this was her. She had come unhinged, just as she feared. No, it was too risky. But Jason had suggested she go away for a while. Lisa. Lisa was safe. She called her sister's number and got her answering machine. She left a message telling her she was thinking about coming for a visit, if Lisa had the time. She put down the phone, her hands shaking. She needed some solid food. That was all. She went downstairs, keeping her hand firmly on the rail.

She prepared a plate of fresh cheese and a salad for dinner, then waited while the French bread heated in the toaster oven. She thought about the things she had never seen and hadn't known she wanted to see. She pictured San Francisco as she set a purple place mat on the white iron table on the patio. She put a hibiscus bloom in a glass on the table and sat down to eat while the sunset pinked and purpled the sky miles away over the Gulf of Mexico. Only a couple of weeks until the end of August. She realized with a shock that she hadn't thought about Gabi and Bryan all day. She would write them a note tonight and send it in a box of chocolate chip cookies tomorrow. She'd tell them she was going to visit their Aunt Lisa. They would probably be glad to see her getting on with something, especially Bryan who had looked really closely at her as the car went down the drive. She knew he felt her fear, and there was no way she could hide from him. Since he was a little boy, he had hurt with the kid in class who was picked on, the old lady in the store where he bagged groceries who was a nickel short, and his mother. No matter how she tried, she couldn't convince him the world wasn't his responsibility. Maybe because he knew she didn't believe it herself.

When Jason came home from his meeting, Maureen was dozing in her overstuffed reading chair with the *AAA Atlas* opened to a map of the Northwestern U.S. A bold red line ran from San Francisco up the coast to Talamook Head near Seaside, Oregon. On the table next to her were sealed letters to her children, addressed in her large, spidery handwriting to their apartment in Gainesville. The smell of brown sugar and butter filled the air. Jason touched her arm. She shifted in her chair, knocking the atlas to the floor.

"Maureen, it's nearly midnight." He bent to pick up the atlas. "What's this? Are you going somewhere?"

He laid the book on the table by her chair and brushed her cheek with his lips, his voice questioning like a visitor at a sickbed.

She smiled up at him. "I'm thinking about it. Lisa's invited me to San Francisco so often. Now, with the kids away." She shrugged. "I thought maybe around Labor Day? Still, I don't know." She touched the book on the table. "It's only a couple of weeks from now."

Jason helped her out of the deep soft cushions of her chair and clicked off her reading light. "Fares are low this time of year. Sounds like it might be just what the doctor ordered."

Maureen turned and faced him in the dim light of the hallway. "I could cook up a few meals, put them in the freezer …"

"Well, actually, I was going to ask you if you minded me joining a group of golfers at Amelia Island that weekend. They had a fourth pull out for some reason." He took her hand. "Of course I was going to ask if you would like to come. A couple of the wives are coming, but I didn't know if the kids would be home or what you had planned." His voice trailed off.

Maureen headed toward the stairs, Jason behind her switching off lights. "The kids will be busy at school. I left a message on Lisa's machine, but I'll call her tomorrow and confirm."

Jason followed her up the steps. "Why not call now? It's early in California."

Maureen looked down at her husband. His face wore a hopeful, nearly youthful, look.

"I won't change my mind, Jason. I'm over the … virus." She stumbled over the word. "But if it would make you feel better, I'll call tonight."

He reached out and caught hold of her robe. "No, whatever you think. Maybe we can put the rest of tonight to better use."

Maureen actually felt the heat of his blush, this forty-eight-year-old man, as he proposed their first sex in months. She squeezed his hand as they entered their bedroom together, her skin flushing hot, then cold—a flash that raised the fine hairs on her neck. She couldn't remember exactly when they quit having sex. After Dylan, it had been a year, though Jason made regular attempts to reach through her frozen senses. Later, they had routine encounters, usually when Maureen had enjoyed a couple of drinks at a party or the kids were gone overnight. Then few and far between became once in a while, and now, they had drifted for months, Jason working, golfing, playing cards at the club, and Maureen? She just seemed to have an infinite capacity for storing things away and ignoring them.

She looked at this man she had once thought she knew, his anxious fingers fumbling with his shirt buttons, and a sad tenderness overwhelmed her. She remembered their first apartment while Jason was still in college, the moon shining through the plastic curtains, the chenille spread on the narrow bed that never seemed too small. She dropped her robe on the chair and felt the cool air caress her flushed body. A different, dormant, warmth curled out of its nest deep inside and spread through her like a cat stretching in the sun.

She moved across the floor, her body leaning toward him, the tips of her fingers, even her hair and ear lobes taut as humming wire. Every part of her was alive, and as she lay down on the bed, she was surprised that the glow of her didn't light up the sheets. Jason leaned over her, kissing her tentatively, like a teenager, then more urgently. His hand stroked her shoulder, then moved to her breast, and she felt as if her skin would become transparent with the swelling of her as she stretched upward into his body, the heat of her like the center of the earth. Jason groaned, and then fell on her, the warm liquid of him spilling over her belly and down her thighs, drained away by the wick of the sheets. He moved away from her, his breathing short and fast, and then she felt his hand on her hip.

"God, I'm sorry honey. It's just been so long … I couldn't control it."

His hand stroked her hip, a short, irritating, repetition. Maureen put her hand over his, holding it still. "It's OK Jason. I know it's been hard on you, too. We can get better at this with practice."

"I don't get it. Maybe it's the stress. My business is getting tougher all the time; lawyers aren't exactly the most admired guys around, in case you haven't noticed. And now, two kids in college at once." His voice took on a hopeful note, and he turned his palm to hers and linked their fingers. "Maybe now, with the kids gone, you could help out? Clarissa is getting really slow. You could take over the bookkeeping at the office like you did when I first started out."

She pulled her hand away. "That was twenty years ago, Jason, when it was just you in the office. I'm not an accountant. Besides, I enjoy substitute teaching and that brings in some money."

"I know that, hon," he said, his voice soothing. "And I know you've been sick. Just think about it while you're out in California. It'd be really helpful, and it'd give you something to do full-time."

"Maybe I shouldn't go if you think it's too expensive. I agree. We are under a lot of financial stress with two kids in school."

"I'm not saying we're poor, Maureen. Forget it. I never know how you're going to react." He rolled over into his comfortable hollow. "I have an early appointment tomorrow. I need to get some sleep."

"Well, I know I need to do more. I've applied for full-time, but they don't need anyone until spring. I could teach piano out of the house for a while. We can talk about it …"

Soft snores answered her. Maureen lay back on the pillow, her body awash in waves of incompleteness and loss. Early on she had lost interest in the short mechanical act her husband called love. When she tried to talk to him about it, he always turned away from her, saying sex was never as good for a woman as it was for a man. Painting his tone was the implication that a good woman would know that. She had bought the latest books and went from draping herself on the bed in black satin to learning belly dancing and surprising him when the kids were spending the night at a youth rally. She cringed, remembering the look on his face, like a father who sees his daughter on the back of a Harley with a tattooed man when he thought she was at cheerleading practice. He had been kind, telling her she was all he needed just like she was, and she just couldn't say that it wasn't all *she* needed. Later on she hadn't shared the ache inside that overwhelmed her in a way she had never experienced as a young woman, and they had gone on, side-by-side, as if there were a clear pane of glass between them.

She closed her eyes, her hand sliding over the stickiness of her thighs into the furnace of her self. She caught her breath and pictured herself in Oregon, high on a cliff. The full moon bathed her in silver, revealing an empty space in her belly, a round disc where the moon shone through. As she watched, the void filled with flame, and she saw herself slowly lift off, her arms outstretched, her hair glowing. She hovered over the Pacific, then spiraled down like a gull, the waves closing over her, steam rising into the night sky.

Maureen waited until Jason left the next morning, then recovered Stephen's note from the pocket of her skirt in the hamper. This time, she left her name and the requested information at the beep. She was mesmerized by Brigit's voice and relieved to only have to talk to the machine. Brigit had to be Stephen's wife. She tried to imagine her, tried to imagine him married to a woman who taught classes on menopause and led rituals. She imagined that she was very exotic with long black hair and dangling earrings. What part did Stephen play in all of this? Surely he didn't teach classes in menopause. Maybe he just kept up the building and stuff. She shook her head in exasperation. Imagining again, putting people in places they never occupied when she actually got there. She wondered what she was getting herself into. When she was sure Lisa would be in her office, she called her. Lisa was already making plans for Maureen's visit.

"I couldn't believe it when I got your message. When are you coming? I can't wait until you get here."

Maureen smiled, enjoying Lisa's excitement. "I have an alternative, Lisa."

"Don't tell me you've changed your mind." Maureen was touched at the disappointment in her sister's voice.

"No, but I heard about a seminar in Oregon for women going through menopause. I looked on the map, and if you have the time, we could drive up together. Otherwise, I'll visit you for a day or two and go by myself."

Lisa's voice sounded guarded. "Menopause? What makes you think I need a seminar on menopause?"

"Not you, me. I know we haven't talked about it, but it's been really fierce."

"Mom called this morning. She said you'd been sick. Did it have something to do with hormones?"

"We can talk about that when I come out. If you don't need it …"

"I didn't say that," Lisa interrupted. "I need to get back to a meeting. When and where is this seminar?"

Maureen filled her in, leaving out the "ritual" part. When she finished, there was a silence.

"Stephen, huh? I remember him. The rugged, silent type. Dad had a fit, as I recall. It's his wife who's leading this?"

"It seems like it." She had a moment of guilt. "Listen, Sis, there's a little more to it than …"

"I've gotta go. You send me the details. I'll get the time off. Time with you is what I need no matter how I can get it. See you soon. I love you."

The phone buzzed in Maureen's hand. Someone else was controlling her mind. None of this was her.

Chapter Four

Maureen awoke to a fully lit day and squinted at the clock in Lisa's small guest bedroom. Noon? She bolted from the bed and took a quick shower, the California blue sky gleaming through the round window. She dressed in jeans and a sweatshirt and hurried downstairs, late for the hair appointment Lisa had made for her, amazed that she had let herself be talked into this. She looked down at the card her sister had left on the table. Jerome. What would he do to her? After all, this was California. The moist, cool air was such a relief from the muggy heat of Florida that even jet lag and a fitful sleep couldn't dampen her spirits. She sniffed the salty Pacific air saturated with the smell of fresh fish. Her step was light as she set out for the shop, Mirror, Mirror, two blocks—or two hills—away. She arrived at a quaint little storefront sandwiched between an apartment house and a parking garage. She waited a minute to catch her breath, then asked the girl seated inside at a small wicker desk if Jerome was ready for her. The girl stared at her, her hand hovering, frozen, over the telephone. Maureen saw herself reflected from all sides, her very female form, her fair skin flushed from the walk, her eyes alert, and that hair blooming around her like an Irish burning bush. She needed a haircut, sure, but she didn't deserve that look of shock. A haunting piece of New Age music drifted from the speakers over the desk, and then, in the mirror, she saw him. A light-skinned, hazel-eyed, black man appeared over her shoulder, in the mirror, his hair an aurora of dark gold. She couldn't unlock her eyes from this twin reflection. She felt a hand on her arm, and heard the soft voice of the south.

"Lisa's right, we could be star crossed," her twin said, and lifted her hand in his. "I'm Jerome, and I'm going to really hate cutting off that hair."

"Maureen," she stammered, leaving her hand in his. She let him lead her to the shampoo bowl, words stuck on the way from her throat.

Jerome swirled a cape around her neck and leaned her gently back, his hand beneath her neck. He wet her hair and slowly smoothed apple-scented shampoo into mounds of bubbles, all the while talking softly about hair styles, natural curly tendencies, how he envisioned her. Maureen didn't register any of it. His lean fingers massaged the thick soap into the hollow at the base of her skull, stroked the back of her neck.

"I guess Lisa didn't tell you about me," he suggested, a smile curling round his voice.

She shook her head no, still not trusting her voice. *A twin*, she thought. *I have a twin.*

Jerome turned on the sprayer and ran warm water through her hair. It soothed her scalp and trickled down her neck. He placed his hand lightly on her forehead to keep the water out of her eyes.

"Maybe she was keeping me for a surprise," he chuckled, his voice wrapping her in the light gold syrup of Grandfather Mountain clover honey. He sprinkled apple scented oil on her hair, then massaged it into her scalp. He wrapped her head in a warm towel, then set the chair upright. "Lean forward toward your knees. You'll be so relaxed, we'll have to wheel you home in a cart."

He stroked and probed from her forehead, around her ears, the joints of her jaw, all the time making little circular motions and humming along with the oboe music flowing from the stereo system. He made his way down her spine, then back up into the base of her skull, the feel of his hands and the sound of his voice loosening the skin from her bones. Without warning, she felt a blooming deep inside, like a lily kept in the florist's refrigerator suddenly exposed to the sun. Heat seeped in a lazy spiral, not surging toward her face like her usual hot flashes, but radiating outward, seeking all the cold corners of her. Warm tears flowed into her lap. Jerome ran his hands down her arms and massaged each of her fingers one at a time.

"You were overdue," he said softly. "Way overdue."

His hands dropped and she felt stranded, wanted this human touch to go on forever. Before she could speak, he handed her a damp towel scented with eucalyptus and closed the curtain around her. She heard his voice fade toward the front of the shop. She sat up straight in the chair to wipe her face and gather herself together. This area of the shop was the only place without mirrors. She was afraid to see herself. She buried her face in the towel and inhaled its fresh scent. So different from that day in Tampa when her world unraveled around her. Had it only been a couple of weeks? She leaned back again, remembering the smell of the hot grass and felt herself slipping away, slipping back to the day Gabi and Brian left for college.

The curtain moved and Maureen woke up, disoriented and sweating. She wiped her face with the still-damp towel. Jerome was back, squatting in front of her, holding his hands up like a director framing a shot. He took her hand and helped her out of the chair. She struggled for composure, then remembered the warmth of this man. She smiled.

"Are you ready?"

She found her voice. "I can't imagine not being ready."

He grinned, and the naturalness of him made her laugh. He led her to a backless stool surrounded by mirrors both whole and fragmented, reflecting herself back in pieces from all directions, her red hair flaring from the ceiling, the back wall, even the floor. She had come apart, just as she suspected. Jerome moved around her, looking at her from every angle, eyeing her body like a piece of art he was arranging. She sensed every place his eyes looked, a connection that was almost visible in the room. She watched him split apart and reform in the mirror, sometimes a piece of him lodged in a shard with a piece of her. He stopped in front of her and lifted a strand of hair that was beginning to dry.

"Obviously we're not coloring, and I can't even imagine you without this hair flaring around you like a flock of copper butterflies. So. A trim, a little shaping and we're done."

For nearly thirty minutes, Jerome silently circled her, snipping and clipping. Tiny mounds of copper wire piled up on the floor at her feet, glowing in the reflections from the mirror. She closed her eyes and waited. Another fifteen and he untied the cape from her neck and told her to open her eyes. He swirled the chair to face the one complete mirror in the room, his hazel eyes glowing with pleasure. She stared at the woman in the mirror, a woman with wide eyes under a smooth forehead no longer draped in bangs. Her hair was a solar corona, circling a face she didn't know, a face of wide cheekbones tinged with color, ear lobes barely showing. She looked like a painting she'd seen once in England, a Venus by Rosetti. She realized her mouth was open and quickly shut it, turning to look at Jerome. Everyone in the shop was standing still, their heads turning first to her then to Jerome then back to her, swiveling like spectators at a tennis game. He stood next to her, their arms touching, and she began to relax into this feeling of belonging, being two branches of the same tree. His eyes questioned her and she nodded.

"I look … I don't know … different," she finished lamely.

"You have something against the word incredible? You look timeless, like a goddess from the old world. What do you guys think?" he asked, looking at the gaping hairdressers and clients.

A chorus of compliments streamed around her like currents, but she was seeing in the mirror what they were seeing—the male and female sides of the same coin. She looked down and saw his arm next to hers. He was the color she turned under the tannin darkened water of the Suwanee river. Next to him she looked translucent and shell-like. He put his hand under her elbow and walked her to the front of the shop, but when she took out her purse he said no.

"It would be like charging myself."

She protested, but in the end, gave in. On the way back to Lisa's, she smelled the grass before it came out of the ground, the roses before they bloomed and the air from the Bay above all else. She was a living wire connected to everything. She let herself into the house just as the phone rang.

"Maureen! Jerome just called. What did you do to him? He wants us to go out later tonight." Maureen heard a strange satisfaction underlying her sister's voice. "He said you looked incredible, and I think stunning was the other word. I can't wait to see you. So, what do you think?"

"I don't know, Lisa. I just got in the door, and I'm out of breath from that last hill." She took a deep breath. "Why didn't you tell me about him?"

"I can't talk right now, Sis. If it's OK with you, let's do it. We have to eat anyway, right? Unless you're not hungry?"

"No, it's not that."

"Shoot! There's my other line."

Maureen hesitated, then decided. "Why not. Like you said, we've got to eat, and I'm leaving tomorrow. What harm can there be?"

"Great. Gotta run. See you around seven."

Maureen stood holding the buzzing receiver. She hung up and went into Lisa's tiny kitchen to fix a cup of tea. She wouldn't think about it, just let it happen. She needed to learn to relax and just "go with the flow" as Bryan said. On the porch of the old Victorian Lisa had turned into a cozy home, Maureen looked over the rooftops. The Bay shone gold in the late afternoon sun, resting in its basin with the graceful arc of the bridge curving over like the handle of a basket. She held the warm cup of tea up to her nose, inhaling the fragrance of camomile and apples. That day when the kids left for school and she started to crack felt like a past life. She had put them and Jason into places marked "later." She was so fully aware of herself that she could feel her pulse.

Maureen shivered as the lights came on one by one across the Bay at Sausalito and the air temperature dropped again. She got up and went inside, turning on the art deco lamps in the living room as she went. Their graceful shapes dropped light onto family pictures in ornate frames gracing highly polished cherry tables. She picked up a portrait of herself and Jason with Bryan and Gabi standing on the steps of the house in Tampa. She was squinting in the harsh light, her hands on the shoulders of her children, while Jason seemed to be looking past the camera at something no one else could see. Lisa had been the photographer that day on one of her trips to Florida—probably Thanksgiving. Maureen looked closer. Was that really her, that flat image with the hair pulled back? She saw herself reflected in the shining table, sending out her own light like a candle inside a glass globe.

She went upstairs and took out the long black skirt and white blouse she'd brought along just in case. They looked like artifacts from a different age. She sat on the edge of the bed, thinking about cutting off the skirt, lowering the neckline on the blouse.

Good God, she thought. How could a haircut? No, she was kidding herself again. It was not just a haircut. For days she'd been like a land mine ticking just under the surface. Ever since Stephen had called back to tell her they had two cancellations, and she and Lisa were on the list, his voice had been in her mind. She'd made an excuse—one even her kids could see through—to see a man she hadn't seen in more than twenty years. Maureen put her hands up to her flaming face. She couldn't even be honest with herself. She was waiting for Oregon, and no matter what happened, she wouldn't go home to Florida the same person. She laid the clothes on the bed and curled up next to them. The teak fan whirred softly against the ceiling, cutting the light from the lamp into streaks of sun filled with tiny motes of thistledown.

* * * * *

"Maureen? Where are you?" Lisa's voice drifted up the stairs, waking her from a sound sleep.

"Up here, Lisa. What time is it?"

Lisa heels clicked down the hall. "Around seven. Are you dressed?"

Maureen looked at the skirt and blouse, now a wrinkled mess under her legs. "I don't have anything appropriate," she answered.

"Oh. Well, I'm sure I must have something …" Lisa appeared in the door, and her eyes widened. "Oh my gosh." She looked at Maureen's hair. "It's wonderful. You look … I don't know. Glowing. More than that. Anyway, you look great," she finished lamely, picking up the skirt from the bed. "Is this it? You didn't bring anything else?"

"It never occurred to me I'd be needing a … what is it I do need exactly?"

"C'mon in my room. We've got plenty of time to go through my closet. Go ahead and look around while I get out of this suit."

Maureen opened the door to Lisa's closet.

"Help yourself," Lisa called from the bathroom.

"No, I'll wait for you," Maureen said, staring at the mini-mall her sister called a closet.

Twenty minutes later she was standing in front of Lisa's full length mirror, a soft white tunic falling from her shoulders to just above her knees, her hair glowing red-gold in the bedroom light.

"It's so short, Lisa," she whispered, turning slowly in front of the mirror.

"Is that all you can say?" Lisa asked.

"I'm sorry, but I'm just wrung out. I don't even know who I am. Today, I found out I'm a twin."

"I'm sorry I didn't warn you. I knew you and Jerome resembled each other, and I thought you'd get a kick out of it. Until I saw you tonight, I didn't realize how eerie it is." She put her arm around Maureen. "Do you mind? I didn't mean to upset you."

"Mind? Oh no, I don't mind. But it's, I don't know. Maybe eerie is a good word. I have these feelings I haven't had in years ..." She stopped and looked at Lisa who was staring at her, wide-eyed.

"Something more than a haircut happened to you, Sis. What's going on? Wait, tell me in the kitchen. We'll get a snack before we go."

Maureen pulled the dress over her head and laid it carefully on the bed. "Lisa, I'm just not comfortable. It's too much like a date."

"Maureen! We're meeting a couple of my friends for drinks. Relax!"

"Well, it's easy for you to say. I've been married my whole life ... something I still am, by the way."

"OK, OK. We'll put one of those big satin ribbons across your chest that says: "Hands off. Married Woman."

In the kitchen, Lisa put some cheese and crackers on the bar and poured the wine. They sat down on the stools in their slips. She looked over her glass at Maureen. "What's going on with you and Jason anyway?"

Maureen took a sip of her wine. "Not much of anything. It's weird. Since the kids left, it's so obvious, but before? I just thought we were a fairly normal married couple and that my husband just lost interest. We were older, he was tired—the usual."

"What does that mean, lost interest?"

Maureen fiddled with her glass. "It means just that—no conversation, no relationship."

"No relationship. You mean no sex?" Lisa stopped, her eyes on her sister. "Maureen? None? Zilch?" Lisa's voice rose, "Why didn't you talk to me?"

"If you're going to start on Jason, this conversation needs to be over. You never liked him, so what would I have said? And Mom? Forget it!"

"You're right. I'm sorry. I don't know why Jason and I never hit it off. Of course, Mom thinks he's the greatest, not to mention no one talks to Mom about anything involving flesh and blood!"

"C'mon, Lisa."

"You know it's true. Besides, I really believed that you and Jason were partners. To tell the truth, I was envious."

"Lisa, I can't go tonight." Maureen paused, her hands smoothing the silk of her slip up and down her thighs.

Lisa's eyebrow cocked in that way Maureen had tried to imitate as a teen.

"Don't look at me like that. I don't know. I'm just not myself. This person, Jerome? He's a total stranger, but he made me feel more than I've felt since Stephen …" She covered her mouth with her hand, tears dropping on the silk and leaving splotches, like impressionist flowers. Please. I'd rather we'd just stay in and we can talk."

"You're afraid! Maureen, Jerome wouldn't. I mean Jerome's …" Lisa stopped, her face flushed.

"It's not him Lisa. It's me."

"OK, hold on. Don't get upset. I'll call him and be right back."

Maureen filled her glass with the tart white wine and drank it down like water, blowing her nose in a napkin decorated with roses.

"It's OK," Lisa said, coming back in the room. "He really seemed to understand. He said to call him when we get back if you feel like it."

"He probably knew I'd back out before I did."

Lisa let that one go. "I'll make us an omelet. Do you need anything before we leave tomorrow?" She opened the refrigerator and took out some eggs.

Maureen took her time answering. "Well, there is one thing. We both need some kind of gown or caftan for the ceremony. I thought maybe we could get something up there," she finished hastily.

Lisa's whisk hovered in the air over the eggs. "What ceremony? You said," she looked at Maureen, "you distinctly said the word seminar."

Maureen avoided her sister's eyes. "Well? Would you have come with me if I said ceremony?" she asked.

Lisa whipped the eggs into a froth and slipped them into the heated pan. "Maybe. I've been kind of looking for a change myself. That Utilities case I told you about?" She sprinkled mushrooms and shredded cheese on the eggs, then folded them over carefully. "It got me a BMW and an ulcer. I thought maybe you could … we could talk … you know?" she finished lamely.

"I guess I didn't get what was happening to you either, Sis. Mm. That omelet smells great. Let's forget all this for now and eat. We've got a whole week to talk, and I'm starving."

Later, Maureen and Lisa settled into the deep cushions of the couch.

"Lisa, do you ever feel like you've just fallen into the wrong movie?"

"God, you've asked me questions like that since we were kids."

"What's your answer?"

"Same as always, I guess. I don't get the question. I just do what I do. Sometimes I'm happy, sometimes not, but I don't think I'm leading somebody else's life."

"Even when things are so different than what you planned? I thought Jason and I would go along side-by-side and end up sharing conversations about the grandkids while we walked on the beach."

"Maureen, you and Jason never did walk on the beach."

"We did in the beginning. You know what I mean. We were busy, and I don't think Jason thought about it. It's like I wrote the script and nobody read it but me. We stopped talking years ago when Dylan . . ."

Maureen crossed her arms over her breasts and held onto her shoulders, shivering. Her voice was barely audible. "I guess that was just the final blow, but I didn't know it."

Lisa took a shawl from the end table drawer and tucked it around

Maureen's shoulders. "I can't believe that for all those years you've kept up this front, this act. I could have sworn you were doing great. Bryan and Gabi are the light of your life."

"That's not an act. I admit I didn't give them any thought today, and that's a first for me. I guess I lived whatever life I was supposed to at the time. But that life's ended now, and here I am asking what's next."

"But you're saying your life with Jason ended a long time ago."

"No, it was just a different life than I bargained for, but I never considered—well, almost never—leaving for something else. The kids needed me. Jason needed me. I knew I'd go back to work after they left for college."

"You don't know how many times I wanted to talk to you about Dylan, Maureen. I just didn't know how."

Maureen hugged the shawl around her. "I've just started down that road. I guess it's part of what brought me here. I don't know what Stephen has to do with it."

Lisa got up from the couch and walked to the French doors opening out to the porch. Fog was beginning to shroud the Bay, but the stars were visible over the house. She spoke quietly into the dark. "I almost got married again after my divorce, but thinking about Dylan stopped me. I knew I didn't have your strength. Then I'd see you with Gabi and Bryan and come home to California unhappy with my life. The night you had Bryan, and the days after when I looked after him . . ." She turned and faced Maureen, her skin luminous in the lamplight, tears pooling in her eyes. "I knew I would be a good mother, but I couldn't risk what you did to do it. I have some regrets, but I chose my role. Lisa Quinn, super lawyer," she wrote on the air, laughing. "It seemed to suit me until lately."

Maureen stretched and unwound herself from the couch. "Whatever we're looking for, I'm glad we're doing it together. It feels good, kind of like a quest."

Lisa hugged her. "There you go again. Are we going to stand around in the woods beating on drums like some feminist Robert Blys?"

"I haven't got a clue. Brigit just said come with an open mind."

Lisa sighed. "OK, I'll work on it. First I'm going to pack and get a good night's sleep. The drive up the coast is spectacular but hard on the driver."

"I'll help."

"Sorry, Sis. A Florida flatlander and the coast road are not compatible—you have to know how to shift and use a brake." She kissed Maureen lightly on the cheek. "Six o'clock alarm OK with you? Breakfast in Sausalito and then on to Oregon." She headed up the stairs. "I feel like we're back in junior high plotting against Mom and Dad."

Maureen yawned, following Lisa up the stairs. "Thanks for today. I'm glad I'm here."

Lisa looked back. "Me too. Just don't expect too much, OK? You always do."

Maureen lay sleepless under the down comforter, the lights of the city filtering through the lace curtains. Lisa was right, she always expected too much and was disappointed. What was it she expected from Stephen? Lisa had seen right through her plan to participate in this ceremony for menopausal women. Was she trying to readjust time, get a second chance to make things come out right with Stephen? That was the thing of movies and romance novels, not real life. She drifted near sleep, the motion of the ferris wheel and the feel of Stephen's hand in hers as real as it had been twenty-nine years ago. She saw them recede toward the barn and the lake behind it, Maureen and Stephen, and then she saw him lay her down on the fragrant grass, the sky spinning above them like Van Gogh's "Starry Night."

Chapter Five

Lisa set down her coffee cup. "Have you heard from Mom?"

They were having breakfast on the porch of the Alta Mira in Sausalito, overlooking the Bay and the Golden Gate Bridge. In the background, San Francisco leaned together on its pedestal, glowing like a topaz in the morning light. Waves with curling foam the color of the fresh milk in Maureen's glass splashed against the rocks of Alcatraz. The sun slid behind a cloud, and Alcatraz loomed somehow more black than grey, the surf pounding dully on the rocks.

Maureen pulled her eyes away. "There was a message from her on my machine just before I left. She was still on that cruise."

Lisa sipped her coffee. "So many memories are cropping up since you've been here. Maybe it's because we're alone for the first time in forever." She hesitated, then plunged on. "I know how angry you are at Dad—and Mom, though I don't understand that part of it. I guess I was just really good at staying out of the way. What I'm trying to say is, I'm sorry I wasn't there when you needed me."

Maureen's eyes picked up the grey of the ocean. "Sometimes Dad set us against each other on purpose, sort of a divide and conquer strategy. Remember when he put boxing gloves on us and told us to fight?" She shivered.

"All we did was cry, poor kids. But, Maureen, that was a long time ago."

Maureen avoided Lisa's eyes, looking around the now empty porch, the chill growing as the sun stayed behind the clouds.

"I'm sorry. I didn't mean to bring all this up, today of all days. But you just seemed to close up when I mentioned Mom." She reached across and squeezed Maureen's hand. "Everybody has a different view of things."

In her mind, Maureen saw the worn and flaking leather on the belt as her dad's arm came down and another welt appeared on her legs, rising slowly like a worm under her skin. She could hear her mother softly closing the door, the click as she pulled it tight, her footsteps going down the hall.

Lisa looked at Maureen and then at her watch. "Let's go. The redwoods are waiting."

*****

The car twisted up the last part of Mt. Tamalpais, and Lisa parked at the entrance to Muir Woods National Monument. The air was fragrant with bay leaf and the thick humid undergrowth. Wisps of mist floated in and out of the tree tops. They walked into the woods, and Maureen stumbled as she looked up. Here was what she had failed to find—the proof of a Creator was in the soaring trunks, the bird call in the ferns. Children spoke in whispers, pointing up where the tops of the trees pierced the mist, letting the sunlight through in slanted rays like stained glass. Maureen stood in the lightning-blasted trunk of one of the oldest trees, stroking the still-living giant with her hand. Peace seeped into her fingers, up her arms and into her center. She tried to imagine what had passed beneath this tree in its lifetime, what it would see in her grandchildren's lifetime. Slowly, she moved on, walking the rest of the path in grateful silence. Lisa was waiting for her on a bench near a slow-moving stream.

"It's unreal here. All the feelings I never found in church are flowing through me. I feel like singing "Amazing Grace" at the top of my lungs."

"I thought you'd like it," Lisa answered, "but that's definitely an understatement. Are you feeling better?"

Maureen sat down beside her sister.

"I'm sorry. It's just like touching an open wound when we talk about Mom and Dad. I hear what you're saying, but I've been mad at them so long it's hard to get out of the habit." She looked around at the golden stillness. "Here it just seems petty, but Mom was so rigid all our lives, and now she's traveling around with men young enough to be ..." Her voice trailed off.

"Why does it matter so much to you? What are you *really* angry at?"

"Oh Lisa! Mothers are supposed to protect their children." Her hand flew to her mouth.

"Oh God, Maureen." Lisa leaned forward on the bench, her face a mask of distress. "You can't think that you ... that somehow you were like Mom? There wasn't anything you could have done to prevent what happened to Dylan."

"I don't know that and neither do you." Maureen twisted her hands together. "I blame Mom for not keeping me safe, but I'm alive and well. Dylan's ..." She jerked her mind away from that place, that square of cheerful green grass laying over the dank hole in the ground.

Lisa looked at her, and Maureen could feel her fear. "Did you ever talk to a priest? Or anyone," she amended hastily.

Maureen shook her head. "I stopped going to church after Dylan's funeral. Once in a while I give it a try—like Christmas Eve or whatever for the family's sake. But it just makes me cry. It doesn't seem to have anything to do with me. Today is the first time I've felt like I could believe again, like I used to when I put the lilacs and peonies on the May altar in our bedroom." She smiled at the memory.

Lisa groaned. "I felt like I was sleeping in a church and shouldn't think about my boyfriend for the whole month of May." She stood and pulled Maureen up off the bench. "Let's go. We have places to go, things to do."

Back in the car, Lisa started the engine and looked over at Maureen. "I remember being amazed at you and how you never backed off like I did. I was eleven when you went behind the altar at St. Xavier's, and you were only nine. Everyone thought I was so tough, and you were the baby with your nose in *Little Women*." She backed out of the lot. "You were really reading *Knights of The Round Table* or something, weren't you?"

Going back down the mountain, the brisk scent of eucalyptus leaves breezed in the window. "I didn't actually go behind the altar, you know. That was one of those stories that grew in the telling." She leaned her head back and took long slow breaths. The smell reminded her of the Vicks Mom had rubbed on her chest when she had a cold. Maybe that was the best she could do given her life—rub a little Vicks, say a little prayer. Maureen looked down at her hand, the same hand that had reached for the huge brass handle in the door of St. Xavier's church.

*****

She'd stayed after school to help Sister Bernadette clean the blackboards and erasers while Lisa had walked on home with her friends. Maureen had really liked Sister Bernadette, a young novice who jumped rope with the fourth graders. That year Maureen was seriously considering a vocation. The convent seemed to be a quiet, safe place to spend your days. That day had been so hot. She'd gotten dizzy standing in the courtyard, banging the erasers against the wall. Sister let her go early, and she had stopped at the church seeking relief from the heat in the dark, cool stones.

The smell of incense and burning candles seeped out and around her as soon as she opened the door. She was momentarily blinded by the deep dark, but soon the blues and greens of the stained glass came through and then the shadowy benches. She dipped her finger into the water that was cupped in the hands of ceramic cherubs, their wrists anchored to the dark paneled wall. She blessed herself and knelt to say a quick Hail Mary. She had felt the silence hum and looked around her. No one else was in the church. That had never happened to her before. Even when she was cleaning out the wax from the vigil lights, Mother Beatrice had supervised. The only light came from the candle in its red cradle suspended over the sanctuary.

She had knelt in the back pew, her knees sinking into the brittle leather cushion and sent her usual prayer forward, trying to wing it upward toward the beautiful face of the crucified savior hanging above the altar. She prayed for her father to stop drinking so her mother would smile, and they could be like she imagined other families to be—sitting down, laughing together—families like the Nelsons, where David and Ricky's father came home and kissed their mother who put supper on the table wearing her nice, white apron. She had prayed to the sweet pink and white face of the mother of Jesus in her soft blue gown, prayed that she would make As and lose weight so her father would be proud of her. She remembered finishing her prayers and squinting at the sanctuary candle, making it flare into shards of light that scattered across the white marble altar that cradled the bones of some saint. She didn't remember standing up, but her hand was on the cold gold gate that separated the communion rail from the altar. Only boys were allowed to serve on the altar—their vestments glowing in the candlelight, their scuffed shoes peeking out below the lace of their white garment. Girls weren't allowed on the altar even to chip wax from the candles. The nuns did that. Somehow they left their femaleness behind when they became brides of Christ.

The heavy gate had swung quietly under her hand, and she stepped through, her pulse thumping against her neck. She could hear her breath go in and out between her teeth. To the left of the altar, across what had looked like an acre of red carpet, was the curtained door where the priest and altar boys entered for Mass. Her body had moved forward, her legs heavy as in a dream, toward the curtains and the secrets they shielded from her. The statue of the Blessed Mother seemed to lean sideways, her shadow flickering in front of Maureen, blocking her way. And then it happened. A voice hissed from the center aisle, ordering her to stop, and she heard the swish of a nun's habit, the click of her beads coming up to the altar.

How she got out she could never remember, but she ran and ran and was found hours later hiding in the neighbor's garage. When Father John came to see her parents, his eyes had looked right through her. After he talked to her father, she thought he looked sorry that he had told on her. That night was the worst beating she had ever had. Each stroke of the belt had come down in a cadence of the bible. The word "sin" timed to the crack of leather on her skin. Five strokes for the five sins he enumerated on her body: envy, curiosity, sacrilege, disrespect, and a last one she didn't hear through the ringing in her ears. She lay on her bed, her whole being shrunk to the pain throbbing in her bottom and legs.

Later, her mother had smoothed Vaseline into the welts. "Your father's right," she'd said. "You'd burn in Hell for touching the altar. Thank God sister caught you early. What in the world gets into you, Maureen? I don't understand why you can't just go along with how things are."

Maureen had lain still under the burning touch of her mother's fingers. She went to confession the next Friday and pretended to be sorry for what she had done, but she had felt a hardening around her heart that only worsened over the years.

*****

As the road opened up and the cliffs sheared away to the Pacific far below, Maureen felt her ribs stretch. Something tight inside her chest unclenched and flew out of her, soaring toward the sun. She imagined her body doing the same, but the seat belt was tight across her lap. She opened her mouth, but no words came out, only the breath she had been holding escaped in a short burst. They rode in silence for miles, the hum of the tires and muted sounds of waves crashing below blended with an occasional car going the other way. Rocky hills and mountain cuts, stippled like a desert chameleon, rose on Maureen's right.

"How do you keep your eyes on the road?"

Lisa's reply was delivered in tones usually reserved for a four-year-old. "Where would we be if I didn't?"

Maureen craned around Lisa, looking down the cliff to the Pacific. "All our vacations were in Florida. Surf like that would mean a hurricane." She settled back in the seat. "One time we went to the Keys. I loved it there." She smiled at the memory. "It has a life all its own, not like the rest of Florida. More relaxing, you know? Barefoot feeling. The kids liked it too, but it made Jason fidgety." She rubbed her arms. "It's the opposite of the redwoods. They make me feel like—I don't know—like I felt when I made my first communion. Key West is more like when you kiss your first boy."

Lisa's laugh filled the car. "Oh Maureen, how I've missed you. Nobody else sees things quite like you do."

"Thank God!" Maureen said, turning her gaze back to the stunning landscape. Huge rocks rose from the surf like herds of giant sea lions. Their wet backs seemed to move as the sun glittered in the spray above them. Further along, sand castle rocks reared up, towering high over the ocean. Maureen covered her eyes with her hands. It was too much.

The sun was blazing on the rim of the Pacific when they found their small hotel on the sea near Rio Dell. After dinner, they walked out on the cliff behind the restaurant. The surf was deafening. As Maureen stretched out to look over the edge, Lisa grabbed her arm.

"Watch out!" she yelled, pulling Maureen back. She leaned close to Maureen's ear. "Sometimes there are weak spots where the cliff extends out over the rocks. C'mon, I'll show you."

A few yards from where they stood, a brick wall ringed a huge hole through the rock. Lisa pointed over the wall, and Maureen caught her breath. Far below was a churning whirlpool with rocks, seaweed and a few pieces of driftwood being sucked down a huge whirling drain.

"You need to be careful. It's like finding your Florida alligators under the lily pads."

Maureen just nodded, shaken by the violent motion of the water below her feet, some memory fighting to the surface. In the room, they took turns soaking in a deep tub, too tired to light the wood in the fireplace. The fog was rapidly sealing the windows as they climbed into bed, Lisa's travel alarm the only light in the room.

Lisa's sleepy voice drifted over the cover. "Maureen?"

"Hmm?"

"Looking for Stephen? It's kind of like you going behind the altar."

"It's not the same."

"Sure it is. You don't know what's going to happen once you look behind the curtain." Lisa yawned. " Maybe it'll be like getting your hair cut. Sweet dreams, Sis."

Maureen lay quiet, luxuriating in the feel of her body uncurled in the middle of the bed, quilts instead of air conditioning comforting her. Jerome's hands had awakened things in her that wouldn't go back to sleep, things dormant for years except for that one brief time with Jason that had ended so badly. She deliberately switched to another track. Lisa's point of view of her, this idea of Maureen as the one with "spunk," as Grandmother Quinn would call it, came as a complete surprise. She remembered her young self as hopelessly romantic, waiting for the time when the lights would dim, the orchestra would slide into a waltz, and her soul mate would slowly materialize across the room. With awe, she read books about women like George Sand and Virginia Woolf, never imagining herself with the courage to exist outside the norm as they did. She wanted to be Jo in *Little Women*. She searched voraciously for the few heroines in history, noting they were almost always disguised as men. Her budding feminism had gone underground when she met Jason.

She closed her eyes and tried counting sheep. In the middle of the field, instead of a fence, was the University of Florida's law library where she had met Jason. She flopped over on her side, plumped her pillows and looked out at the moving grey against the windows. She thought how that was her. Everything she wanted black and white answers to came up grey, even her dreams. She pulled the quilt up tight against her chin. That's what Lisa was trying to tell her about Mom. She really would try harder, she thought, as the smell of wet leaves and mist filtered down the chimney. The smell was just like Gainesville that November so long ago.

*****

Most of the other students had been at the stadium watching the football game, but Maureen was going to the law library. She had a paper to do, and a law student in her class told her she'd find what she needed there. She climbed the steps of the brick building that would have been comfortable at Oxford, huge oaks towering over its ivy thatched walls. Inside the heavy doors, the library had felt more like a chapel, sun pouring in through the stately windows and flowing like honey over the polished wood tables. Maureen sat quickly near the door and pulled out her notebook with the reference booklist. Suddenly, into that hazy, dreamy, bee-buzzing afternoon came the sound of drumming. It was like soldiers' boots coming closer and closer, a thunder rolling from the front of the room toward the back where Maureen sat. She had been frozen in place, the men at the other tables looking right at her, their feet thudding on the floor. She felt her heart beating in her neck, skipping like a trapped moth in the hands of a child. Then their hands had joined in, beating palms down on the tables. What was it? What terrible thing had she done? She had somehow gotten to her feet, knocking her papers and her pen on the floor and escaped out the front door, her breathing harsh and loud against the bare trees and cold air.

Maureen sat under a tree, sat hard as her knees just quit holding her up. The sound gradually died, and she realized she had left all of her belongings in the library. Oh, but she knew she could never go back in there. It was then that the door opened and a slight dark-haired boy a couple of years older than her came through and down the stairs, his face flaming as he tried to juggle her purse and her notebook with the flower cover. He came over to where she sat and laid her things on the ground, then squatted next to her.

"Are you OK?"

She nodded.

His light brown eyes searched her face. "I thought everyone knew." He frowned. "On the other hand, most people don't have to I guess, except the few women law students." He paused. "Are you a law student?"

She shook her head.

"That's good, seeing as how you don't have a voice." He helped her up.

She cleared her throat. "Are you saying . . ." She stopped, started again, "Do you mean women can't go in there?"

"Yes. That's what I'm saying. It's not written, just understood. All law students know though."

She thought of the student in her history class who had suggested she come here. He probably thought it was a great joke.

"I have to get back to my books. Are you sure you're OK?"

"Yes. I'm fine. Thanks for your help." Maureen gathered her things together, then saw the tips of his brown shoes still standing there. She looked up.

"I didn't introduce myself." He stuck out his hand. "I'm Jason Manley."

She had shifted her books to her other arm and shook hands with him.

And that was that. It was as if they had met in war time, everything moved so fast. Jason seemed so sure of himself. He was totally estranged from his family, so she didn't have to pass muster with anyone but him. He just assumed control, and it was a relief for Maureen to accept his guidance, to put her daydreams away. Her mother and dad had been thrilled. What they had imagined for her had not come to pass. They dated until Maureen finished her degree, then married. She'd gone directly into teaching while Jason got his law degree. They had few highs or lows, just a steady, comfortable life. Maureen loved teaching music in the junior high school. Then came Dylan and Gabi and the rest of her life.

*****

Maureen pulled her feet back under the quilt and untwisted her nightgown from around her hips. She hadn't thought in years about how she and Jason met. Amazing how that one smell of autumn brought it all back. God, they had been so young, so hopeful. Sleep finally stilled the thoughts careening around in her brain. Later that night she dreamed that she was swimming in an underground cave, her red hair glinting in the clear water, small fish swimming through her fingers. In the back of the cave was a cleft with something gold wedged in it, something her dream self knew was important. As she tried to swim forward, the tide surged back out of the entrance, pulling her with it, swirling her down into the darker blue water where the coral waited. The mouth of the cave receded, then closed, and she felt a monstrous grief. She cried out in her sleep.

*****

At breakfast the next morning, they marked the map Brigit had sent them. Afterwards, they sped up the coast highway, the fog burning off like angel hair lit from behind by a candle. They were still in redwood country, and both seemed content to stay silent. They stopped for lunch, but each was curiously quiet, like they were preparing themselves for something.

It was nearly dark when they arrived at Emania Lodge, a beautiful A-frame of glass held together with cedar poles. They pulled the bell hanging outside, and a lovely sound, like one that used to call monks to prayer, echoed down the walkway. A tall woman answered the bell, wiping her hands on an apron. Her long, silver hair was bound up in a bright yellow scarf.

"You must be Maureen and Lisa," she said briskly, ushering them in.

Maureen recognized the voice as Brigit's, the one from the machine.

"You're the last two in, so it was an easy guess. I hope your trip was pleasant?"

Maureen heard Lisa answer the pleasantries. She was speechless at the view, the glass at the rear of the house seeming to leap into the sky, no ground visible from the front. She felt Brigit and Lisa behind her.

"It is breathtaking, isn't it? We've been here for years, but I never get used to that view as you come in the door." Brigit headed for the stairs that floated up on the right. "I'll show you to your room, and then I need to get back to the kitchen. We can talk later." Her head disappeared over the banister. Maureen's mouth watered at the smells coming from somewhere in the house.

They followed Brigit upstairs where she showed them their room. Behind her, the scent of cinnamon drifted. And that wonderful voice. "Go ahead and bring your things in. The bathroom's at the end of the hall. We'll see you in the dining room in a half hour."

She had said "we." Maureen didn't want to see Stephen. Not now. Not tonight. She couldn't imagine what she'd been thinking. Her stomach was tied in knots.

Brigit came back up the stairs. "Stephen's out of town—we're all women tonight. Wear something comfortable," and she was gone again.

There were twelve of them at dinner plus Brigit. She went over the schedule for the next day as Maureen gazed up into the night sky that sparkled through the glass ceiling. The house was built around a central core, a long peaked room containing the living and dining area surrounded by glass. On the north wall was a mammoth fireplace cradling a blazing fire that warmed the stone floor. Colored Indian rugs were scattered around the huge room creating bright oases of chairs and tables.

"Is your food OK, Maureen?" Brigit asked.

Maureen looked down at her plate where her food sat untouched. "I'm sorry." She tasted the vegetables, a wonderful spicy combination. "Mmm. This is great."

Lisa passed her the fragrant bread. "Wait until you try this."

Maureen didn't look up again until her plate was clean. Brigit served hot apples with cinnamon, telling them to make themselves at home. They would meet for breakfast at eight o'clock.

"Breakfast," Lisa groaned. "I'll never eat again." She stifled a yawn. "That reading chair in our room looked really inviting. If you don't mind, I'm going to go on up."

"Help yourself. I'm going to look at the surf, and then I'll follow you." Maureen patted her stomach. "That was the most wonderful salmon I ever ate in my life. Brigit's not only beautiful, she's a great cook, too."

Lisa studied her. "Well, you always knew Stephen had good taste. You shouldn't be surprised."

Maureen glared at the sting of tears in her eyes. "What an idiot I am. What did I expect? That I'd come waltzing in here after twenty some years, and he'd be waiting at the door to throw himself at my feet? I'm an embarrassment to my kind."

Lisa put her arms around her sister. "C'mon. Tomorrow he'll be here, and he'll be bald and pot-bellied. You'll be telling Brigit she's too good for him."

Maureen rolled her eyes. She grabbed a jacket from the stand near the door and headed out, Lisa's laughter rolling down the stairs. She inhaled the cold foggy air. The surf boomed from behind the house as she followed a stone path around the side. She cut through a small garden, her hand brushing stone walls that seemed to enclose some sort of interior garden, but she didn't see a door. Herbs scented the fog that was growing heavier around her as she walked up the cliff on stairs made of granite slabs. The wind was so strong off the Pacific she could practically lean on it, like a living wall. The smells of salt, iodine and fish were thick as incense. She breathed it in and sat down on a rock, cradling her arms together under the jacket as the night air turned colder.

What *was* she looking for here? At the least she and Lisa were getting to know each other again. She shivered. No. It was more than that. And it wasn't just Stephen, though thoughts of him had triggered all of this. It was herself she was looking for. The self she had believed in when she was young and that she had lost along the way. When she had opened up to Stephen, it had been really hard. She had learned at a young age to shut down. Then, when he disappeared from her life, she had vowed to never open up to anyone again. But she had. Not so much to Jason as to motherhood, that trusting nameless love that flows between mother and child. And then, Dylan. Now she was inching toward it again, and she was scared. Not just nervous, but terrified, like she was moving toward something she wouldn't be able to manage. Something that would change her into a person she didn't know. She groped for the right thought, the thing she was most afraid of. And then she knew. She was afraid she wouldn't fit into her life any more and would have no idea where to go or what to do. All the labels were on crooked—Jason's wife, Gabi's and Bryan's mother, Eleanor's daughter.

She shivered, looking up at the vastness of the sky, the stars showing through breaks in the fog. She would be fine, she thought. She just needed night to turn to day, and she would be fine. Going back, she took the path around the north end of the house and saw shadows leaning toward one another in what Brigit had called the studio. She breathed on the window and wiped it with her sleeve. Inside, sculptures stood and lay in seeming disarray, their shapes eerie in the moonlight filtering through the fog and the misted windows. One looked like two people with their arms around each other, another like a winged horse. She heard a footstep on the path behind her.

"That's Stephen's studio," Brigit said, her steady hazel eyes shining. "He's quite a wonderful sculptor. Right now, he's in Portland doing a show."

Maureen rubbed her hands up and down her arms. "You must be really proud of him."

"We all are. The idea of making a co-op out of artists with such different interests was scary."

"There are more than the two of you?"

"Stephen shares his studio with a potter in the winter. I run the seminar portion, and sometimes there are one or two women here in training with me." Brigit put her arm around Maureen. "You look frozen. Let's go in by the fire."

Brigit brought mugs of mint tea to the scarred and battered table in front of the fire. "This table is what Stephen calls a 'found piece.' He found it floating off the coast and cleaned it up. I think it came from a ship's cabin. What do you think?"

Maureen looked at the wood burnished gold by the fire. "Oh, I don't know. I think it might be from a table some family was bringing to the new world from Europe, maybe meant to be part of the family dining room."

"That's much sadder than the cabin idea. Stephen was right. You do have a soft heart."

"He talked about me?"

"Of course. When you called, he told me he hadn't heard from you since high school. He was excited that you were coming." Brigit yawned. "It's been a long day and tomorrow will be longer. I'm headed up. Do you need anything?"

Maureen shook her head. "No, thanks."

Brigit stood with her hand on the railing, her face glowing from the heat of the fire.

"Stephen should be back the day after tomorrow. He'll be anxious to see you. Sleep well."

Maureen sat for a while longer, sunk deep into the huge chair. She wondered what Stephen had told his wife about her. Certainly not enough to bother her. Reality was a damnable thing. Brigit was a nice person. She blushed, remembering her daydreams here in this woman's house. She'd written a poem in her journal called "Night Gardening," an erotic piece about fruit and seeds and laying vines down. A man enters the garden. She remembered the first line: "There is a stirring going on in a neglected glade."

The heat rose from her neck to her forehead. Maybe she needed to leave with Lisa, go back to San Francisco tomorrow after the ceremony. Her plan to stay later seemed foolish now, a high school scheme. Her eyes closed as the fog rubbed up against the windows and the coals burned down in the fireplace. Sometime later, she went up to bed, the soft snores of Lisa making her smile before she fell into a blessedly dreamless sleep.

Chapter Six

A fire scented the air with juniper and cedar as the twelve women sat on straw mats, their hair lit by the last rays of the sun. Brigit threw a handful of dried herbs onto the fire. The aroma of mountain and sea swirled upward in the smoke and curled around them. Amidst the sound of pipes and the soft thump of a small drum, a trio of older women entered the clearing. The song they played created a haunting sense of timelessness. Maureen swayed where she sat, dizzy from the darkness, the fire and the scent of the air. A woman swirled a gourd filled with beads so tiny they swished like the surf as she moved it over the heads of the seated women. At Brigit's urging, all twelve stood, joined hands and stepped slowly around the fire. Maureen felt the world slip backward, sensed the wolves abroad in the night, their eyes watching. The trees around her became part of a dense forest covering the whole continent, mosses and ferns releasing their scent into the air. Her breathing was deep and rhythmic as she swayed to the beat of the drum, her hand in the hand of her sister.

A deep voice began to chant, a voice like Brigit's, but infused with a rich darkness, dark as old blood. The women in the circle felt the power of the earth through their feet, the power of their bodies through the hands of the women at their side. The drum and pipes played faster, and they moved like they were children again, loose-limbed and feeling their bodies without shame. When the drum slowed, Maureen's mind fluttered reluctantly back to the clearing, a bird stopped in mid-flight. Her breathing was loud in the silence.

Brigit stood near the fire, her shadow flaring on the trees and wavering against the dark.

"We are all here for the same reason," Brigit began, as Maureen sat closer to Lisa. "We come to celebrate one of the most joyous and holy times for women. In years lost in the past, it was called the blood-wisdom time. Women welcomed the pooling of their blood inward. They didn't fear it as some of you do." She looked around the group, holding the eyes of each woman. "No longer do we flow only outward to nurture others. We need our strength to nurture ourselves. Then we can pass this knowing on to younger women."

Maureen felt Lisa's shoulder lean into hers, and she thought of Gabi, a world away in Gainesville. Brigit's strong voice rose and fell around the fire, drifting into her ears on the scented smoke. Maureen felt the beginning of the familiar hot flash rising up her chest, bathing her face. Brigit turned toward her.

"The heat all of you feel is symbolic of the burning out of the container, the strengthening of the vessel. Don't fight it," she urged, her voice rising. "Become part of the heat."

The muffled beat of the drum began again, and Brigit swayed slowly back and forth, her voice falling into the rhythm of the storyteller.

"I have a tale to tell," she began, the fire painting her face the color of a winter sunset. "It's a tale of courage for all of us who are afraid."

The sound of the wind skimmed over the small drum, and the rain drifted inside the gourd as Brigit's voice dropped lower. Maureen could feel her skin tighten, the small hairs on her neck stirring.

"This story was told by our ancestors to their daughters and from them to their daughters, until, for a brief time, the tale was lost." Brigit sank to the ground, closed her eyes and raised her face to the dark sky. In a voice that carried to each ear, she began to tell the legend of Flamia.

*****

In the time before time, the oldest daughter of the clan of Cherok was offered for sacrifice by her father. This choice would elevate him in the Council of Men. His wife turned her back as the sign was carved into the ankle of her daughter, Flamia. She smeared her face with ashes and covered her ears to the cries. From that day on, her voice did not answer to her daughter.

Early one morning, on a day when the sun had refused to reveal itself and the sea met its twin in the flat, grey sky, Flamia was taken in a boat by her father to be left on the island where the god lived. As the day wore on, Cherok strained to keep going, his aging body streaked with sweat, his breath coming in little spurts. Flamia begged him to change his mind, take her back to the village, but his flat eyes looked right through her. Late in that strange pewter-colored day, they arrived at an island and went ashore for water. Cherok handed his daughter a bowl and pointed toward some high dunes. As she went toward them, a howling arose from the nearby forest that seemed to come from the bowels of Mother Earth herself. Flamia turned, her eyes wide like those painted on the shields of the warriors. She saw her father, rowing away.

She threw herself into the water and swam after him, her arms making jagged splashes as she frantically chased the boat. She reached it and grabbed hold as the shrieking and wailing pierced her ears. Her father struggled to pull away from the island, his eyes wild, his face white as the death hag. Still, Flamia hung on, even as the boat reached the swells beyond the reef. Then, her father grabbed at his small ax. He swung it high and chopped down at his daughter's fingers, severing each one. They fell into the water, where they turned into little florescent fish that swam beneath the boat and disappeared. Cherok saw none of this. All he could think of was escaping the clutches of the island and getting home. Even then, Flamia did not stop. As the moans from the island carried across the water, she hung on with her bleeding palms, pleading for her father's mercy. Again, his dull ax hammered downward, severing her hands at the wrists. Her palms tumbled over and over, transforming into flat fish that floated in the grey sea like opalescent porcelain bowls.

As Flamia fell away from the boat, her blood flowed down to the shelf surrounding the island, forming the most delicate of pink coral. Her father rowed with all his remaining strength into the open sea. By morning he was back in the village, all trace of his daughter washed away in an early morning rain. The village prospered that year. A ceremony was held to honor the sacrifice of their eldest child by Flamia's father and mother.

In exactly one year, less a week, Flamia's two sisters were out fishing for their father's dinner. They didn't have their minds on their task but had managed to catch a few fish. The eldest sister, Gala, was to be given to the god on the coming full moon. The sisters had become so close after the loss of Flamia, that they could not believe what was soon to happen. Never before had a family sacrificed more than one daughter. Their father was going to be the next chief because of this. Their mother had turned her face to the wall of their hut and had not spoken since the announcement was made, one month earlier. The sisters did not question, for it was as it had been all their lives and forever before.

The soft purples of twilight touched the waters. The youngest sister wrapped their fish in wet palm leaves. Suddenly, the water around them swirled into sucking pools and wild winds appeared from nowhere, pushing their boat further into the sea and away from their village. All they could do was hold on, each hidden from the other in solid sheets of black rain that slammed closed their eyes. As suddenly as it began, the storm ended. The sisters saw that each was safe, though the clothing was torn from their backs and the hair matted to their heads.

Across the now calm waters, the nearly full moon rose, blood red and close enough to touch. Just at that precise moment, the boat grounded itself. Growls and moans of torment erupted from the nearby trees, tearing the silence. The sisters tried to push the boat back into the water, but it was stuck tight. They were so tired. As they clung together, the youngest saw a hut down the beach. She suggested they offer their fish to whoever was in the forest and run for the hut while he ate. Without waiting for an answer, she stepped from the boat and laid the fish on the shore. As she did, her eyes locked onto the empty eye sockets of a skeleton laying there.

All who tell this tale agree that they could not have recognized the skeleton as their sister, Flamia. Her flesh was long gone from her bones, her eyes eaten out by the fish, her heart and liver the diet of crabs and other scavengers.

Little sea creatures had attached themselves to her bones and her long flowing hair. They were luminous in the moon's light, like pearls and opals. The sisters were so afraid. They were frozen in that spot, holding tightly to each other. At their feet, this fearsome pile of bones. In the forest, the raving beast. Then, a strange thing happened. Gala felt her heart ache with pain for the skeleton laying on the dark sand. She saw the arms ending at the wrists and cried aloud. She couldn't imagine who would do such a terrible thing.

The yellow eyes of the beast peered at them as he roamed the edge of the wood, but he made no move to come closer. And then Gala knew the bones of the woman protected them. She picked her up, the long sparkling hair dragging over one arm, the leg bones dangling over the other. The youngest retrieved their fish, and slowly they made their way down the beach. The moon lit their path as she slid higher and higher in the sky, leaving a highway for them to follow.

When they reached the hut, Gala sucked in her breath and stumbled, nearly dropping Flamia. Over the door she saw the sign that was carved into her ankle. The beast who roared from the trees was her destiny. She laid her burden down inside the door, the bones clattering and clinking on the packed dirt floor. The moon shone in, and she saw the faint scratches on the ankle bone of the woman. They matched hers! Here was one who had escaped, but at what price? Her tears fell on the water-smoothed bones of Flamia's cheek. The youngest sister stood in the door, hesitating, until the roar of the beast shook the stoop and she flew inside, slamming the door behind her. In the corner lay an animal skin, and she helped lay Flamia on it, covering her against the chill night air.

Gala struck her flint, flaring light on a fireplace filled with dry wood. When the flames were strong, she lay the fish across the wood. As the scent went up the chimney, the cries of the beast turned to whimpers. The youngest went to the door and listened. She heard the trickling of water and the strange, melancholy cries from the forest. She filled shells with water while Gala watched over the bones of Flamia, laying them out in a seemly fashion. Then she placed the small fish and the fish shaped like porcelain bowls on palm fans.

After they had eaten, Gala said a prayer to the gods over Flamia, her tears dropping on the fragile bones of the chest just over where her heart would be. For a moment, she thought there was flesh on the cheeks where her tears had fallen earlier, but a shadow passed over the moon and the vision was gone. The younger sister left a plate of fish and some water next to Flamia as an offering. Her tears splashed onto the arm bones of the woman. For a moment, she thought she saw the rose of flesh on her chest, but a cloud passed in front of the moon and she knew it was her imagination. Then she laid a flower where Flamia's arm ended at the wrist, and her heart ached as her abundant tears washed over the hip bones and leg bones cradled in the soft fur. The sisters agreed that beast or no beast, in the morning they would give her a proper burial. They lay down together in the corner, keeping each other warm with their young bodies as the fire died.

They slept the sleep of exhaustion and innocence.

Moments later, Flamia opened her mouth. She sang a sad, crooning song that reached deep into the dreams of the sisters. Tears came to their eyes, though they didn't waken. As she sang, more flesh began to curve her form, her hips becoming lush and broad, her belly round and full, her breasts rising like the moon from the sea. The flashing opals became the blue-green of her eyes. Soft lips formed over the smooth ivory of her teeth. She sat up and greedily drank the water they had left. Then she ate the fish. As she did, the palms of her hands appeared below her wrists, sweetly curved. One by one, her graceful fingers grew, as supple and pink as a newly born child's. By the time the sun rose again, Flamia slept as herself for the first time in nearly a year.

The sisters awoke to the sound of birds and saw Flamia asleep on the skins, her cheeks a healthy pink, her hair shining in the sun's light. They cried aloud with joy as they recognized her. Flamia awoke. She hugged them and touched their skin with her restored hands. Then, haltingly, she told them her story, the story of their father's betrayal. Her sisters listened, eyes wide with horror. When she finished, Gala told her the village had been safe and prosperous this whole year. Her father said it was because of the sacrifice of Flamia to the beast. Now, they knew the terrible thing their father had done, the lies he had told. And yet, he had offered another in his greed.

Flamia snorted in anger. How foolish they all were! They must make sure this didn't happen to anyone, ever again. Then, despite the fearful protest of her sisters, Flamia left them in the hut and went into the woods with their one remaining piece of fish. They heard her soft singing and the growls of the beast throughout the day. They prayed and sang songs for Flamia's safety. That night, just a bit of the golden light of the moon was left behind when Flamia left the woods. The huge beast walked at her heels. His shaggy head swung from side to side as he looked fearfully at the sea, but he continued to follow her.

Flamia, her sisters, and the beast lived on the island until their deaths, the beast having grown quite fond of fish and fruit. Every year, a new girl joined them, and they danced in the light of the moon. They raised flowers and vegetables and harvested the unusual fish found only in that sea, the fish shaped like slender fingers and curved palms. They kept the old boat hidden behind the wellhouse, just in case.

*****

The drumming stopped, and in the hush of the woods only a far off owl could be heard. Brigit opened her eyes. "Women used to know these things. Until you have faced death, until you have lost everything, you cannot know life." Maureen heard murmurs of assent all around. "We all live on the surface," Brigit continued, "We fear going into the unknown, the down under where we will find ourselves by losing ourselves. Until Flamia faced the truth, the nature of her father and her own desires, she could not live."

As she spoke, several women came into the light of the fire, their red robes glowing. "All of us have been where you are," Brigit said. She sat down behind Maureen. The others, except for one tall elegant figure, sat behind the other women.

"I, too, was lost in the depths like Flamia," the tall woman said. "I needed to face what I had been avoiding. In my case, it was me." She turned her face toward the fire. A shiver ran around the group as they saw the scar tissue layered around her mouth and eyes. She turned back toward them. "I was so afraid of getting old! I spent everything I earned trying to stay young. I had surgery on my face, my breasts, my thighs. I could always find doctors willing to operate, but the choice was mine. After my second eye operation, my system started protecting my eyes with layers of new tissue. The more surgeries I had, the worse it got. I stopped going out in public. It took me a long time to face myself." She smiled. "But I have, and I didn't do it alone."

Another woman told of the fear she experienced after her husband's death, her desire to take her life to be with him because she didn't know who she was without him. Others described battles with cancer, fear for their children on drugs and their feelings of responsibility, the rejection of divorce in middle age. Then Brigit stood again. The drumming floated toward the fire, the soft whoosh of surf and trees building in the background. Brigit lifted her arms over her head, and her gown slid down and pooled at her feet. A sound like winter wind moaned in the circle as the fire licked the scars where her breasts had been and flamed on the sickle-shaped gash below her belly. Slowly, she moved, the grace of her body and the flickering fire turning her scars into painted ritual markings. Brigit danced the story of Flamia, going down and then lifting herself, telling the story of her mastectomy. Maureen saw the knife, felt its edge, the parts of Brigit's body dropping into metal containers. One by one, the other women joined her, bodies of every shape and size, scarred and changed by childbirth, beautiful in the firelight. Maureen wept. She felt as old as time and as young as a new flower. She was aware of every part of her self in a joyous recognition. She could have danced forever, but the drums stopped as women began to drop out, some of them sitting quietly holding the woman nearest to them. Brigit put on her gown and sat down, sweat glistening on her face.

"I have something to say," Lisa whispered, her hand holding tight to Maureen's. Her hand trembled, and then Maureen could feel her gather herself together. "My sister went through the worst thing a woman can go through—her child died before she did. It's a thing you never expect, like a sin against nature. Then, I went through the worst thing a sister can go through—being unable to help. I loved Dylan, my godchild." She took a deep breath. "I loved him with all my heart and I love Maureen, but I couldn't get through. She shut all of us out and went where no one could touch her, and she took Dylan with her."

Maureen felt tremors shake her, felt her bones crack and her muscles rearrange themselves. A fist clenched where her heart was and she couldn't catch her breath. Lisa just held on tighter and continued to speak.

"Maureen and I are going through menopause at the same time, but we were going through it alone. She had given birth to her three children. I assumed she'd just be glad to have all of this over with. I couldn't tell her about my grief. How could she possibly understand how I felt knowing I would never have a child?"

"Oh, Lisa." Maureen's anguished voice floated on the breeze.

"That was, until tonight. Now I think I know that the same applies to all of us. We hold everything down deep and only visit it by ourselves. We turn inward or we wall up our insides and turn outward with this half-a-woman face. It's the same even if we're sisters and mothers, like the mother in Brigit's story turning her face to the wall."

"Yes, yes, it's true," voices chimed in from all sides.

"That's all I want to say, I think," Lisa said, looking at Maureen. They held each other, tears mingling on their cheeks..

"I think that's enough for tonight," Brigit said quietly. She stood and folded her mat. "Each of you will be spending the night in a tent with your partner," she began.

Questions flowed from around the fire. Brigit held up her hand. "Everything you need will be provided."

Maureen remembered the forms she had filled out asking everything from what she slept in, to any medications or dietary needs. She gave Lisa a small wave and followed Brigit into the woods. Near a quiet stream, a white tent nestled in a hollow. The night was quiet, like a church at midday. Only an occasional rustle in the grass broke the silence. Brigit held back the tent flap and Maureen saw sleeping bags on the ground, her favorite nightgown folded on one.

"Is there a bathroom?"

Brigit handed her a roll of tissue and pointed into the woods. Maureen felt foolish, like she had broken some kind of spell by her need. When she came back, the woods dense and dark in the hours just before dawn, Brigit was sitting cross-legged on her mat, eating an apricot, a thick blanket wrapped around her. Maureen put on her gown and sat quietly.

Brigit gestured to the fruit, nuts and water sitting on a small camp table. "The ceremony takes a lot of energy. Please, help yourself." She studied Maureen as she ate, the dim candlelight flickering off the sides of the tent.

"I want you to know that we draw lots for whom we will guide," she said, looking closely at Maureen. "When I drew you, I told the group it might be a conflict since you have a past with Stephen."

Maureen drew back, and Brigit immediately reached out to her.

"I was just worried that there might be something you wanted to share that you would feel hesitant about since I know Stephen. Anyway, the group said there could be a specific reason why I *did* get you in the draw."

She wiped the apricot juice from her fingers and snuggled deeper into the blanket. Maureen waited expectantly.

"Is there anything you'd like to ask me?"

Maureen shook her head. She should have been tired, but she buzzed with energy.

Brigit opened a pouch and laid strange looking leaves in piles on the table. For the next hour she showed Maureen how to use herbs for the symptoms of menopause.

"Are any of these good for calming down feelings?" Maureen began, then stuttered to a stop. "I mean, well, you know. Sexual feelings?"

"Why would you want to do that?" Brigit asked. She looked amazed at the question.

Maureen shifted uncomfortably. "I can't explain it. It's like I'm on 'ready' all the time." She felt the heat warm her neck. "I feel things I never felt when I was younger. Stronger feelings." She shrugged, her palms up. "I just can't explain."

"You just did. What's the problem with all of that?"

"My husband, Jason? All of the sudden, he just couldn't care less." Maureen told her, haltingly, about her last encounter with Jason.

"It sounds to me like you don't need to turn yourself off. Jason needs to get some help."

Maureen shook her head. "Jason thinks he's fine. He says it's my problem. He wouldn't even consider counseling."

"Maybe you've done all you can," Brigit suggested softly.

"Would you give up on Stephen?"

"You have the wrong idea about Stephen and me, Maureen. We're friends and associates. Stephen has someone else," she added, looking strangely at Maureen as if just putting her finger on something. "Someone none of us around here has ever met. I do know he's never married."

Maureen didn't know what to say.

Brigit turned down the blanket on her sleeping bag. "I think this takes more time than we have right now. Let's sleep on it and talk about it tomorrow."

Maureen rolled and turned, her body lit up like a torch, her mind roiling with the things she had heard and seen.

She felt Brigit's hands on her back. "Just relax. I'll give you a massage to help you sleep." Her hands felt like small animals, soft and yet strong underneath.

"You're getting tomorrow's lesson on massage early."

"I tried my usual meditation," Maureen said, relaxing under the gentling of Brigit's hands. "But I can't seem to clear my mind with so many things to think about. "

"Have you ever tried using your animal guide?"

"I've read something about it, but it sounds so 'new agey.' Just taking yoga and learning to meditate was far out for me. I have a hard time concentrating."

"None of this is far out for you, Maureen. You could lead all of us if you'd let go."

She laughed as Maureen turned rigid under her hands. "OK, let's just try a little experiment." She finished massaging Maureen's feet with a cream that smelled of fresh mint.

"Oh," Maureen sighed. "That was heavenly."

"Just relax. You came all this way. You might as well trust me. If you can't do it, you can't. First, you have to find out who your spirit guide is. I'll send you off to sleep with a spirit guide meditation. When the guide comes to you, just let it lead."

Maureen was nearly asleep already and could barely nod. Brigit told her how to think about the animal world and ask for what she needed. "Everyone has an affinity to one particular animal. Everyone. From the Celts to the American Indians, all the people know we have a connection to the animal world."

Maureen didn't hear the rest of the instructions. She was already dreaming herself walking on the beach. In her dream, Maureen was coming from behind the rocks near the sea when she saw something at the water's edge. It was a beautiful woman with long, brown hair and dark skin, smooth and sleek. As Maureen moved closer, she could see that the woman looked sad as she leaned out over the water, and there was a strange, mournful sound in the air. Maureen felt something in her hands and looked down. She was holding a bronze colored pelt so soft it seemed to nestle in her palms like a kitten. She had found it in the rocks, but she knew that it belonged to this woman. She went down onto the beach and held it out, calling to the woman until she turned. The sun sparkled off the tears on the lashes of her huge brown eyes. She saw the skin and held out her hands to Maureen, the sadness deepening on her face.

"Why are you crying?" Maureen asked, her voice hollow in the dream.

"I left my children behind in the sea when I became human. They are calling me. Can't you hear them?"

Maureen listened. She heard mournful music coming across the sea. It was so human, she could feel her heart breaking.

"I have been gone too long. They need me."

Maureen went closer and saw that the woman's skin was dry and beginning to peel off of her in long strips. She handed her the skin and watched as she put it on. As soon as the woman pulled the skin up her legs, she began to change. She walked out into the water as she smoothed the skin over her head, the long hair gone, the body falling forward into the sea. As she dove under the waves, a tail flipping into the air, two children came running down the beach calling for their mother. They cried so long and hard, their tears swirled around Maureen's feet, and then she felt their hands clutching at her legs. She heard the seal-woman crying as she swam out to her other children.

Chapter Seven

The day after the ceremony, the lodge vibrated with energy. Several women mixed herbs while Virginia supervised. Others were learning how to teach their partners massage. It was evening when the other women finally drove off, reluctant to leave this place. Only Maureen and Lisa remained with Brigit and Mary Virginia, and Lisa was leaving in the morning. Maureen had never known the company of women in this way. She was reassured, like she had touched a sacred stone. As she fell asleep under the down cover, Maureen felt like she was in two worlds—one real, one shadow. Tampa was blurred and very far away.

The next morning, Lisa woke her early. "Let's walk before I go."

They walked quietly for a few minutes, and then Lisa took a deep breath, like she'd made a decision. "You know I love you, Sis."

"Of course I do." Maureen stopped walking. "What's this about, Lisa?" She looked at her sister and a grey fog touched her spirit. How she was going to miss her.

"I'm just worried about you. I can't imagine you going back home and taking up where you left off."

"Lisa." Maureen hugged her sister hard. "Of course I'm not going to. Sure, a weekend is a pitiful spit into the wind compared to a lifetime of habits but don't worry. I have two days to work on this before I fly home."

"Well, I just wanted you to know that I'll be available if you need to talk or if you need anything at all." She hesitated, then the words fell over one another as if she feared she wouldn't say them if she didn't hurry. "I'm already making some changes myself, but I'm afraid I'll slip back without help. I've been writing down everything I think about this as it's happening to me. It helps, but I'll need to call on you, too. What do you think? Like the buddy system we had during the A-bomb drills."

"I'd like that." Maureen felt a wave of affection for her sister, the tough career woman who had never needed anyone.

Lisa looked at her watch. "See? I'm leaving two hours later than I planned. I'm already a different person." She got that silly look she'd had as a kid. "Race you back to the house?"

Maureen laughed through the sadness clotting in her throat. "I don't think so. I'll walk a little longer."

"I love you, Sis." Lisa held her tight. "And thanks for bringing me along." She walked back to the house.

Maureen watched Lisa's car disappear down the road, the taillights winking in the mist like miniature lighthouses. She turned her face up to the rain. It fell so softly in Oregon, not like Florida where she would be soaked and dripping ten feet from her front door. Here it was like a skin treatment, a mist from a gentle sprayer. She walked along the bluff a way she hadn't come before and nearly stumbled into one of those worn away parts of the cliff Lisa had shown her down the coast. She shivered as she looked down into what appeared to be a new break, rock fragments sticking out like sharks teeth. The water seemed far below and churned like the devil's washing machine. As she watched, the water and debris receded, exposing a solid rock shelf. Maureen shivered, backing away as clouds passed over the sun and the rain turned chill. She hurried back to the house where lights were coming on in the welcoming rooms.

That afternoon she read a book purely for pleasure, a well-thumbed edition of the children's book *A Wrinkle in Time* by Madeleine L'Engle. As she moved into that other universe, she wondered why children accepted things with such open hearts while adults fought it all the way. She closed the book late in the afternoon, accepting that she, too, had entered another universe. One she would have a lot of trouble abandoning.

She showered before dinner with water so hot the steam rolled from under the door and built a mist in her bedroom. She dressed carefully, wearing the bronze colored skirt and sweater Lisa had helped her buy when she realized a Florida wardrobe wouldn't do in Oregon. In the bedroom light she shimmered through the fog, her hair like flames around her flushed face. Stephen's arrival lit up inside her like sunset on the Illinois prairie. She walked downstairs, unaware of where she placed her feet.

In the dining room, Brigit was removing a setting from the table. She took in Maureen's flushed face and looked down at the plate she held. "Stephen won't be here for dinner. His show is going really well, and he's wrapping up some sales."

Maureen's glow faded.

"But he said he'd be in this evening, just later than expected." She touched Maureen's hand. "Would you bring in the soup?"

Dinner was quiet, only Maureen, Brigit, and Mary Virginia, the tall woman with the scars. Like a curtain parting, Maureen realized that Mary Virginia was Brigit's mate. She felt her senses as if she could see them vibrating just beyond her in the shadowed dining room. Brigit smiled. The candles flickered over her face, her thoughts flowing down the table to Maureen like the soft rain against the windows.

"She knows," Maureen thought. "She knows I'm waiting for Stephen."

After the table was cleared and dishes done, Brigit passed Maureen on the way upstairs. "I'll see you in the morning. Just remember. Nothing happens that isn't meant."

Maureen stiffened. How could she be so sure of things? She hadn't … then she remembered her at the fire, the flames leaping over her scars. She put her arms around Brigit. "Thank you," she whispered back.

The house was silent when Maureen curled up in one of the big worn chairs near the fireplace and covered her legs with a cobweb soft afghan. She picked up a book from a table spilling over with poetry. She flipped the pages and saw the numbers identifying poems by Emily Dickinson. Her lips moved silently as she read number 249.

Wild Nights—Wild Nights!
Were I with thee
Wild Nights should be …

A clenched part of her between the base of her spine and her belly opened into warmth. She closed the book, leaning her head back on the chair. Even you, Emily, alone in your room in 1861. What was it you really wanted? She heard the back door open and close. The only sound was the crackle of the fire. Maureen's ears strained toward the kitchen. Silence, then footsteps and finally, Stephen stood in the door. She wouldn't have recognized him in a picture, but she knew him as she knew her own children. He had a beard and his hair was longer, but he leaned in the doorway the same way he had leaned against that building at the State Fair more than twenty years ago. Maureen felt that same yearning fill her chest, like a wildflower stretching toward the sun. And then he was in front of her. He put his hands on the arms of her chair and sat back on his heels, the irises of his eyes reflecting the flames from the fire, missing nothing about her.

"I would have known you anywhere," he said, his voice a deeper, fuller sound, as if a trumpet had turned into an oboe.

She cleared her throat. "I …" She began again. "You've changed."

His eyes questioned her. "And?"

"I would have known you anywhere," she said, hugging her arms across her chest.

He touched her hair, briefly, a wing's brush. When he lifted his hand from her, it was as if she were thirsting, and the glass of water was taken away. She touched his face. His beard was like that pelt she had held in her dream, dense and silken. His eyes met hers, and she dropped her hand quickly, as if she'd been burned.

He moved away from her and gestured around the room. "How do you like Emania?" he asked, his voice too loud for the space they had created between them.

"Oh, Stephen, I love it." She tasted his name on her tongue, a name unsaid for so long. "I can't imagine not being here. It's like my real life doesn't exist outside this space." She hesitated. "Actually, I've decided that it's enchanted."

"Oh, but it is. Didn't Brigit tell you?"

There was an awkward silence.

"How much longer will you be here?" he asked.

"Just tomorrow. I have a flight back from Portland the day after." She smoothed her hair. "I'm sorry you missed Lisa."

"So am I, but the reaction to my show was so much more than I expected." He paced the room. "It was my first exhibition at this fancy gallery in Portland. They say it's a tough audience." He dropped down in front of her chair on the thick Indian rug. "I sold everything. The owner was thrilled. He planned this big reception for tonight."

He sounded sixteen.

"Why didn't you stay? It would have been good for your career."

He looked at her, the same look she remembered from so long ago, the one that reached a hard place deep inside her and made it stir.

"Why didn't I stay?" He looked disappointed, and she knew why. She was playing a game. The social game.

Maureen felt the heat of a major flash rising from her chest into her neck. She was lightheaded but remembered Brigit's instructions. She laid open hands on the chair arms, breathing deep into the heat.

"Maureen, are you all right?" Stephen had come onto his knees in front of her.

"I'm fine," she said, and she was. It had worked. She was back to herself.

He settled back on the rug. There was an uncomfortable silence, both of them lost in memories, trying to find a place to start. Finally, Stephen spoke, his voice faint against the crackling of the fire.

"I think of you every day. When your son died, I cried for you every day. It was as if I had lost a part of myself. And yet," he struggled to compose himself. "I knew I didn't have any rights to your feelings, to your life. I felt like a spy, but I couldn't stop."

"How did you know what was happening to me?"

"Lisa. She came back for her high school reunion. I was home for my dad's funeral, and we ran into each other downtown."

"Stephen, I'm so sorry."

"He lived longer than he should have," he said shortly.

"Lisa! I can't believe it. She never let on." Maureen put her hand to her burning cheek.

"She made me promise to not get in touch with you. The only time I broke that promise was when your son died. When I didn't hear from you, I knew I was supposed to stay out of your life."

"She must have put it there," Maureen said quietly.

"What?"

"Nothing." She touched his hand, tentatively as a child. "I just found the letter you wrote all those years ago. It's why I came."

The silence was back, both again in their own thoughts.

"But now you're here. What do we do about that?"

Maureen didn't answer. Truly, she didn't know what they would do about that. Stephen took her hand and pulled her up from the chair. "I want you to see my studio. We could wait until morning, but it's really different in the moonlight."

Maureen hesitated. Some of the lessons of Emania were taking hold in her heart, and one of them was that she needed to learn to depend on herself, love who she was, not wait for some other person to come along and make everything all right. But this was Stephen, not just some other person. She stood in the circle of his arm, smelling the rain and woodsmoke on his jacket.

"I've looked in the windows," she began, embarrassed.

"What did you see?" he asked, his eyes probing her face.

"Just shadows, shapes. Nothing I could identify."

His hand was rough, but he held hers gently, like a fragile teacup. They went through the dark kitchen, lit only by the pilot light on the big old gas stove. The house sighed as they went out through the back door and across a stone terrace, their footsteps muffled by the wet leaves. Stephen turned a key in a heavy wooden door and stepped back. She went ahead of him. A memory shook her to her soul. This was the secret garden, the place in a book she had reread twenty times as a child. The moon was behind the clouds, but it filtered down through the glass ceiling. The soft hiss of the rain added to the quiet. Stephen turned on a yellow light, creating a halo around a luminous sculpture. It was a man and a woman, entwined in such a way that you couldn't tell where he began and she left off. Maureen forgot to breathe. She couldn't take her eyes off of it, even though Stephen had moved on and pools of light were dotted all over the studio. He came back to her, a questioning look in his eyes.

"Maureen?"

She stroked the marble, a creamy white with veins of deepest rose rising up the stone. "I always believed in your art. I'm just so grateful that you went back to it after ..." She stopped. She realized she didn't know after what. After he walked away from her? After he took her trust and threw it away? She really didn't know anything about him at all. She looked up at him, but the words didn't come. She walked through the studio slowly. Some objects were still just blocks. Others had figures emerging like mermaids from waves. She stopped in front of a piece of marble the color of cliff roses with a figure rising from it. She tried to imagine what it would be.

"Brigit calls them my 'middle agers' when they're at this stage."

"I can see that." She touched the warm stone. "What is this going to be?"

"I don't know yet. I'm waiting for it to tell me."

Stephen's eyes were on her, those same eyes etched with fine wrinkles. Then she felt his hand at the small of her back, warm and somehow familiar. What was she doing? She hadn't thought this far. Nobody but Jason had touched her in so many years. She felt weak, as if she would collapse into a pool of clothes and boneless flesh if he should take his hand away.

"I need some air," she said, heat rising up her neck. "Does this door go outside?" She pushed on the door.

His hand dropped from her. "It does. It goes to my meditation garden. We can go back the way we came if you're ready." His voice was flat, hearing an answer where she had given none.

"I'd like to go in the garden, if you don't mind." She leaned on the door, suddenly in need of clean air, marble dust thick around her.

He stood silent for a moment, then shrugged as if he'd made a decision.

He opened the door from a spring above the frame. A wall surrounded the space except for a small door in the far side. Grape vines wound so thick overhead that the rain didn't penetrate. She could see where someone would assume it was part of the house and never notice it. She had passed it herself just this morning, put her hand on the wall. As her eyes grew used to the dark, she saw a small lily pond with stepping stones, a bench and a statue in the far corner. She continued standing in the door, leaning on the frame, afraid to move. A match flared and candles bloomed like lilies on a low stone table. Stephen went back into the studio, brushing by her as he brought out two cushions and laid them on the bench. She felt electricity where his clothing had touched hers. He led her forward and she sat gratefully, inhaling the moisture into her lungs. Stephen stayed standing over her, his hands tense by his side. The heat and anxiety drained out of her. She felt calm, her thighs relaxing on the cushion, the misty air bathing her face.

The candles flared on the statue, and she thought she was looking at a modern pietá. She peered closer. No. It was a mother and young child. The anguish in the gracefully bent back of the mother took her breath away. She felt Stephen sit next to her, his warm hands enclosing both of hers. She was still looking at the woman, seeing her head bent closely over the quiet figure of the child. The child's face was turned into her breast, and one tear lay on his cheek. The candle flared again, and she saw the features of the woman. Her heart stopped beating, then resumed its rhythm slowly, agonizingly. It was her own face, sorrow etched in the marble like a prayer.

"Oh, Stephen." Tears gathered, flowed down her cheeks. So many tears! Where did they stay, waiting all these years for release? "How could you have known?"

"I put how I was feeling for you into the woman. I never meant for you to see it." His voice cracked as he took his hand away from hers.

"Oh, no. To see it is such a gift! To know that someone else knew what I was feeling."

"Surely your husband knew what you were going through." He faltered on the word husband. "And your mother?"

She shook her head slowly, remembering the sense of being isolated in a bubble of air, nothing touching her. "We all knew only what each of us was feeling." She tore her eyes from the child and leaned back against the wall. "Except for Lisa," she said softly. "Lisa always knows how I feel. And now I know there was someone else." Tears continued to flow, dropped into the palms of her hands and onto her lap like baptismal water.

He put his finger under her chin and lifted her face to his, then gently kissed the corner of her mouth where the salt of her gathered. He traced the arch around her eyes with his artist's fingers. She felt the calluses on his palms as he weighed the bones of her face with his hands. She had come home. The other part of her, missing for so long, was sliding into place like the final piece of tile in a mosaic picture. She had been a desert without a stream, functioning but not blooming. His hand moved to the back of her neck, cradling the base of her skull like a vase of flowers. His mouth tasted of salt, and she knew the feel of his skin, the smell of him. She needed to feel him along the whole of her, know the fit that she had always sensed was theirs. The desire to feel his skin against hers, nude as the marble of the statue in the studio, shuddered through her. As if in a dream, she lifted her sweater over her head, the trembling candle flames painting her breasts copper. She heard his breath catch in his throat as he laid her gently on the cushions, as one would lay a young child down for a nap. Tenderly, as if he were touching peony petals, he undressed her and then himself, laying their clothes like an offering in front of the sculpture. The scent of seaweed rose from his shoulders, and all around them the mist and fog drifted in the candlelight. Their skin wore delicate drops of moisture. His hands knew her, had sculpted her from stone, and she lifted toward him with a cry of recognition. She was night-blooming jasmine, all fragrance and waxen petals opening to the rain. His cry matched hers, floating out of the garden and joining the calls of seabirds riding the Pacific currents.

Later, he covered her with a blanket from his studio. He stroked her hair, then her face. Neither spoke but fell into dreamless sleep curled into each other.

*****

Maureen awoke to the sound of birds, and saw Stephen standing over her with a mug of coffee, smiling down at her like a little boy at Christmas.

"Good morning."

She reached up to smooth her hair and felt his hand on hers.

"Don't. It's right like it is." He put the mug of coffee in her hands, and she felt the warmth feed through her fingers and up her arms. The smell was wonderful. Had she ever really smelled coffee before? He sat down next to her.

"What do we do now?" he asked, finally, tucking the blanket in around her legs.

"The first thing I do is take a warm shower," she said, smothering a groan as she sat up and wrapped the blanket tight around her. She handed him the mug. She tried not to look at him, tried not to see that expression of love that left her feeling fifteen and longing, even though her back was stiff and her legs creaky from the damp bench. "Is there another way in?"

"It's only six in the morning. No one else is up. Maureen, I …"

She put her hand on his mouth.

He took her hand away, kissing her fingertips one at time. "OK. I'll wait while you shower, but after that we have to talk." He held her still. "You need to know that I looked for you, and when I found you, you were married. I would have given you anything, but I couldn't give you children."

She touched his face and nodded, not trusting her voice. She pulled the blanket around her and looked down for her clothes. They were stacked neatly in a little pile on the bench. Without warning, she laughed, joy lifting her.

"What?"

"I don't know. Here I am, the same Maureen, a married woman with children, and yet I'm not her. I'm so filled with happiness. I just need some time." She picked up her clothes.

"Not too much time, Maureen. We've lost too much already."

She saw him smile as she left. His eyes were full of her and something else, the slightest tinge of fear, as if she would disappear.

After her shower, Maureen rubbed the towel over her freshly washed hair. Her mind was racing. Finding Stephen signaled a new life. They belonged together. That set so many things in motion that her head was full, tumbling thoughts chasing each other like waves on the beach. Gabi and Bryan weighed heavy on her heart. Jason would do fine. She was sure. She occupied such a small part of his life. Maybe he would find a woman who shared his love of sports and understood the stock market. But Gabi and Bryan counted on them for continuity, something she had always promised them. Still, they were off on their own now, and they were no longer children. It was time for her to find her place in this new room in the house of her life.

She put her hands to her head, hoping to stop the thoughts from running into each other, looking for some clear direction. She wanted to meditate. She thought of Stephen, and a smile curled itself around her mouth, her heart lifting like a lily pad on a still pond. She tiptoed downstairs and heard Stephen and Brigit in the kitchen. Biscuits were baking. Her mouth watered. But first, she would go meditate on the bluff. Stephen would understand. There was no doubt they would be together. How to do it was the question.

The fog thickened as Maureen neared the ocean, the surf booming far below. She looked around, puzzled, her smile fading. She must have missed the path. She wasn't paying close attention. The fog swirled at her feet, parted briefly to reveal the rocky coast, then closed again. She heard a muffled voice calling, but the fog tricked the ear so she couldn't tell which direction it was coming from. She'd better go back to the lodge. Brigit had warned them about how quickly the fog could move in, but she wouldn't have been able to imagine this. She turned back the way she thought she had come, and the earth opened underneath her. She hit her head as she slid through the jagged rocks, felt herself flung like a rag doll into the freezing whirlpool below. Some far-away part of her observed that she hadn't told Brigit about the break in the cliff. She could hear her name as the water closed over her head, the pain erased in the ice-blue cold. She heard the voice of Stephen pleading for her to stop and wait for him.

*****

She was falling, but without fear, lightly, as if she had wings. The frigid water turned her blood to shards of crystal, piercing her heart, before the surf pulled her out and under, into a soothing blue warmth. She felt solid, sleek and powerful as she spiraled deeper. Others escorted her descent, their skin gleaming in the purple light cutting through the midnight waters. Her breathing was one with the water, the rocks, the seals that called to her in their mournful human voices. She gave up to the unknown, floating alone into a familiar cave, her eyes flared like anemones. The walls of the cave trembled and leaned inward as the tide surged, licking up the rocks like tongues of cold fire. A whirlpool pulled her backwards, swirled her toward the entrance that was slowly filling with the tide. It was then that she saw him suspended in front of her, the water around him shimmering, his long hair caressing the tenderness of his neck and shoulders. She knew the rightness of it—Dylan here with her as she learned to breathe water. She cradled the answer to her long unspoken question; she knew he had not suffered as she had not. Love flowed from him to her as his gentle face began to waver and then become translucent. Even as she opened to him, she knew he was telling her to go back. She felt the powerful pull from above as she struggled to stay connected to him, even as the walls of the cave tumbled inward.

Her silent cry trembled above him. "I came to be with you!"

The light around him swam forward, surrounded her in comfort, filled her mind with the presence of Gabi, Bryan, Jason, her mother, Stephen. She sensed others calling to her, many others, their voices blending with the seal's call. Oh, how she understood the wrenching decision of the seal woman. She slid away, watching his light become more and more concentrated until it just disappeared, leaving only that part that glowed on her skin. Maureen was dragged upward by a force she couldn't fight. There was incredible pain tearing at her as her lungs were forced to give up the sea and return to the air. Then, nothing. Blackness enfolded her and cold, deep, dark cold, turned her bones to blue ice.

*****

Maureen opened her eyes to the frigid, white smell of chlorine, stinging fluid from a thin needle leaking into her pale arm. She turned her head awkwardly toward the sound of snoring, the tube in her throat pulling tight. Jason slept on a chair, his jacket wadded behind his head. Her mother, her paper thin eyelids bathed by the rising sun, huddled inside her Chanel suit on the recliner. Maureen shuddered and struggled to go back to her dream. She had been about to hear the music beneath the water that she had strained toward all her life. The secret Dylan would tell her about herself. She could almost hear it, his voice, whispering to her.

"C'mon, Maureen. Open your eyes. Please."

She clung on tight, trying to find her way back to that safe place but finally gave it up. She peered through swollen eyes and saw the fear-shadowed face of her sister next to the machine that was breathing for her, its soft whoosh the surf that had invaded her dream.

"Thank God." Lisa leaned closer, touched her hand softly. "I knew you could hear me," she whispered.

Maureen's eyes flickered toward the chairs.

"Don't worry. I'll tell them you're back with us when they wake up." Lisa's cool, strong fingers opened Maureen's hand, placed a smooth stone in her palm. "Stephen said to give you this." She straightened, her fingers lightly brushing Maureen's forehead where one small pink spot showed amid the bruises and abrasions. "He saved your life you know."

Maureen's eyes stretched wide, the anguish of trying to communicate radiating from her.

Lisa heard. "Don't worry. He's fine. A little banged up but fine."

Maureen looked down. A water-washed stone nestled in her hand. She curled her fingers around it, and raised it to her nose slowly, her arm sending signals of pain through her whole body. She inhaled the scent of the sea. Looking toward the chair where the sun glared off the lines etched around Jason's mouth, she drifted off to sleep, clutching the stone in her hand.

Chapter Eight

Jason and Eleanor stayed for a day after Maureen regained consciousness, but they were frustrated by her inability to communicate. Lisa persuaded them to go home since she had taken an extended leave from her office.

Maureen was moved out of intensive care the morning after her mother and Jason left. Stephen came down from his room and sat in the chair by her bed, holding her one good hand in his one good hand. Maureen searched his face.

"It's hard to tell how you're doing with those black eyes," she said, her voice gravelly from the tube they had removed late the day before. Her words faded in and out like a bad microphone. She tried not to cry as she looked at the yellow-brown bruises covering his face. She was so weak. The tears came as easily as breathing.

"And for a minute I thought I was in Greta Garbo's room," Stephen responded.

"You mean my new sexy voice or this turban?" Maureen moved her head slightly, groaning. "I thought I'd had headaches in my lifetime, but I'll never complain again."

"I heard that," Lisa said, coming into the room. "And there's a witness." She touched Stephen on the shoulder affectionately. "It does my heart good to see the two of you together again." She cleared her throat.

Stephen stood slowly, the arm and shoulder cast making his movements awkward. "It was a little … strange before. Your mom wasn't exactly thrilled when she figured out who I was, so I made myself scarce."

"I'm sorry I missed that," Lisa said, her voice shaded with sarcasm.

"Lisa." Maureen shook her head at her wonderful stubborn sister, then winced. "Mom's in a state of total confusion right now. This is the first time I've seen her actually looking her age."

"I know, I know. And it was good of her not to fill Jason in on Stephen. I promise," she said, picking up Maureen's free hand, "I'll be good."

"I need to get out of here and let the two of you talk," Stephen said, limping towards the door. He turned back to Maureen. "Lisa and I have been getting to know each other for the last few days. You were right about her." The door swung closed behind him.

"What did he mean by that?"

"I told him how awful you are," Maureen said. Her voice faltered, and she waved her hand helplessly. "I want to talk to the kids, but I can't keep my voice going. Lisa? How about you call and I'll put . . ." Her words ended in a raspy squeak.

"The doctor said it would take time to get your voice back to normal, Sis. Don't worry about it. I've talked to Gabi and Bryan several times. We told them the bare minimum: you fell, your leg was broken, and the tube you needed for a few days kept you from talking."

Maureen smiled at her sister, happiness a glowing presence in her, alive as Dylan had been in the cave. He hadn't suffered. He'd shown her.

"Maureen? Are you OK?"

She came back from her memory and nodded, grimacing as the heavy bandages pulled on what was left of her hair.

Lisa tried to plump the flat hospital pillow. "I'm going to San Francisco tomorrow, but I can come back anytime you need me. The doctor said you'll be a few more days here, then they'll release you to Brigit and Stephen for rehab at Emania."

Maureen's one eyebrow went up.

Lisa nodded. "Yes, Jason and Eleanor agreed. Obviously they can't see to it themselves. Brigit has a license as a physical therapist and so does Jerome. He'll be coming to spend a week with you." She turned toward the window. "Actually,

I'll be bringing him up."

"Ah hah!"

"What do you mean, 'ah-hah'?" Lisa demanded. Just then, the nurse came in.

"OK, Miss Quinn, I need the patient for a while." She turned to Maureen, thermometer in hand. "It's nearly time for your pulmonary therapy."

"Saved again." Lisa kissed Maureen on the cheek and went out the door.

Maureen hated the appearance of the young man who smelled like cigarettes. His machine was supposed to help her lungs work properly. Her lungs had begun to work on their own, but they were still weak and what the doctor called "bruised," though she had a hard time imagining that. The therapy hurt like hell, but she would put up with anything to get out of the hospital and resume her life. It was going to take all her courage to face Jason and tell him her decision to move to Oregon, but she had never been more sure of anything in her life … not since she rode the ferris wheel back in the summer of 1960, thirty years ago.

The therapy session ended midafternoon. Maureen fell into a fitful sleep, her body throbbing in every joint, her chest aching as if someone had beaten on it with a mallet. Slowly, her body calmed, and a blue-green mist filled the hospital room. Her body fell away as she floated to and through the ceiling, the roof of the hospital receding behind her. Music of a kind she'd never experienced resonated all around her, bringing a sense of water, seals and Dylan.

As a child, she had sometimes held her breath in the lake and gone under, turning in slow sensual circles until she felt her head and her feet were connected, and she was an organism that survived in water. This time, she knew she wouldn't run out of breath. Ahead, behind and around her were others like her, formed and formless at one and the same time. A sense of Dylan, a sense of her father, passed through her like bubbles. Without effort, she absorbed their thoughts and the knowledge that she would not have been who she was, would not have done the work she was doing and about to do, without the experiences of their lives and their deaths. She felt her energy compact as she accepted these truths, and suddenly, she was back in her bed, awakening from her sleep, cool and refreshed.

She sensed someone in her room and opened her eyes, expecting Stephen. A slight man with greyish-blue skin sat next to her bed, his collar identifying him as a priest. She groaned inside and closed her eyes, feigning sleep. Her eyelids began to quiver convulsively after what seemed like at least fifteen minutes, and finally, she had to open them. He was looking slightly over her head at the screen that blinked and bleeped and kept the nurses informed that she was still alive.

"You're a lucky woman," he said, his voice perfect for the priesthood—warm, deep, resonant.

She nodded slightly.

"Your mother …"

Maureen turned her head, made eye contact with him. His eyes were blank screens, like a television that's not turned on. She shivered. Her mother. She should have known.

He cleared his throat, his voice a little less sure now. "Your mother said you couldn't speak yet, but she felt you would want to take the sacraments." He extended a narrow, perfectly manicured hand toward her, then withdrew it as he observed her bandages. "I'm Father Nicholas. I'm attached to the hospital here, so you can reach me anytime." He stood. "You seem tired. Perhaps I'll call on you again tomorrow."

As he left the room, Stephen came in the door. The priest waited for Stephen to shift one of his crutches, then shook his hand. Maureen heard the words "sacrament" and "anytime" floating down the hall as Father Nicholas went looking for others who might be more cooperative.

Stephen sat next to the bed, his hand resting gently on the sheet over Maureen's thigh. "You look so tired. I can't wait to get you to Emania."

At the thought of the lodge, a smile lifted the edge of Maureen's mouth. "When?" she asked.

"I didn't make out the word, my love, but your eyes are full of it. As soon as the doctors say yes."

"When?" she asked again, louder this time. Her voice was getting stronger by the moment.

"Next week. If we can talk them into earlier, we will, but it's your lungs.

Your leg isn't the problem. We can immobilize it on the trip. Just keep doing those breathing things, and we can go."

Maureen blinked back tears. Damn, she was so weak here in this bed.

Stephen dabbed at her eyes with a tissue. "You're human, Maureen. No one could have come through this the way you did. You deserve a few tears."

The flow was interminable. She had cried a lagoon of tears this past week. Where had she kept them all these years?

Stephen mopped her face, smiling at her with a love so clear it hurt to look at him. She was so afraid it would go away. "How can you look at me that way after what I put you through? You could have died."

He bent over and kissed her ear lobe. "I wanted to, if you did."

Maureen shuddered. "Don't say that. Please." She'd finally found him and then almost lost him again.

"Next week we'll be home," he said. "Then you can cry all you want."

"Then I won't want to," she whispered, turning her head just enough to kiss his knuckle where it rested on her cheek. She tried to tell him about her dream, her new knowledge, but he shushed her.

"We have plenty of time. Save your voice." She fell asleep again, his finger stroking the only available skin on her face.

It was two more days when Maureen finally talked to him as she had wanted to talk to Jason. While Stephen held her hand, she told him about Dylan. She recalled the joy he took in all of life, his trust that rebuilt her faith in the family, a faith she had lost as a child. As she talked, the loneliness receded like a wave leaving the beach. Dylan's life re-formed in front of her as she shaped it in the words that would create him for Stephen. She saw the smile that had lifted her heart, the young, strong legs carrying him across the lawn, the look of awe on his face when she brought Gabi home from the hospital. He had been little more than three years old, but he'd drawn the blanket back from Gabi's face gently with one freshly scrubbed finger. "Sister," he'd said, love and wonder filling his voice.

Stephen squeezed her hand. "You can talk some more tomorrow." He gave her a glass of water.

"No, I want to do it now. Don't you see? No one would say his name. It was as if he never existed. He curled up in the bottom of my heart, and I only talked to Gabi about him. Then I stopped, because Mom said it was morbid and selfish."

Stephen looked at her with such tenderness. She felt her heart healing. "How could you be selfish? You were trying to help your daughter hold on to his memory."

"She said it hurt Jason to think about it, and it made Gabi sad. I guess I wasn't thinking straight, so I listened. I put him away like a keepsake in a box."

She stroked the back of Stephen's hand, memorizing it. "I kept you in the dark like that for so many years. Now I have both of you out in the light. It doesn't seem possible."

He kissed her forehead. "You won't lose either of us, ever again."

Maureen lay back on the pillow. "You know, the things people said were so amazing. They didn't mention Dylan because they didn't want to upset me. Even Lisa. As if I had forgotten, and they would cause me pain by reminding me. How is it possible that good people could think that way?"

"Are you really asking?"

Maureen nodded, searched his face. "Yes, I'm really asking."

"I think they meant well but didn't have the right words for something so monumental. So they convinced themselves you'd be better off to keep Dylan buried. Most people are afraid of emotions so they ignore them or let Hallmark say it for them. But people like you? We need your help to open doors to ourselves and experience life."

"Me? No, I don't think so. Brigit. She's a door opener."

"She is, but so are you. I think that's what Dylan and your father were trying to tell you in that dream." Stephen looked up as the nurse came in the room. "Uh-oh. The cops."

The nurse rolled her eyes. "You have to go, you know. Your nurse thinks you've skipped town."

"I keep telling you. Just put me in here. I'm good for her."

"Talk to the administrator." She put the thermometer in Maureen's mouth. "Meanwhile, boys over there, girls over here."

Stephen hobbled to the door, blowing two kisses back into the room: one for her, one for the nurse who was too busy changing her dressing to notice. She grimaced as the tape pulled on the stitches.

"You know," the nurse said, "all of us think you two are the most romantic thing since Romeo and Juliet."

Maureen felt the heat rising up her neck, and this time it wasn't a hot flash. Rumors flew around a hospital as fast as germs. Jason had been here, signed all her paperwork as her husband. What must they think of her?

"I mean, the way he saved your life? It's like a movie. You owe him a lot."

Maureen nodded, sleep overtaking her as the nurse adjusted her i.v. Just as the dark pulled her in, she heard the nurse's words echoing, "… so lucky …"

Lucky? Maybe. Blessed, for sure. She had been given a chance. She started a prayer but was asleep before the words formed.

Stephen chuckled to [illegible] back into the [illegible] one [illegible] the time [illegible] was too busy [illegible] dressing to notice. She [illegible] at the [illegible] pulled on the [illegible]

"You know, [illegible] I think you're [illegible] the [illegible] romantic thing since Romeo and Juliet."

[illegible] Renee's [illegible] paper [illegible] What [illegible]

[illegible] the way [illegible] you [illegible]

[illegible] nodded [illegible]

[illegible] that [illegible]

[illegible] had been given [illegible]

[illegible] for her [illegible]

PART TWO

GABI'S STORY

Chapter Nine

In the small, airless building that served as an airport for Gainesville, Florida, Gabi waited for her grandmother. Her mind leapt like water beads on a hot pan from one event to another. Her anticipated college life had evaporated into a numbing series of soap opera scenes. Her grandmother was coming to live with her. The news hardly made a ripple since she was trying to cope with the horror going on in Gainesville, and her mother's accident in Oregon.

Classes had just started when they found the first body. This guy, the murderer, was really frightening—bone-chilling creepy, like stories they told each other in the woods during Girl Scout camp. The things they say he did to those girls was something Gabi tried not to think about, but they kept coming up in her dreams. The police said he might be a medical student since he seemed to display some kind of skill with a knife. Gabi wondered why they didn't think he was a butcher. Her worst nightmare was the one with the girl's head spinning around on the stereo turntable. Maybe people made that up or saw it in a movie, but Gabi couldn't blot it out. It replaced the dream she had of Dylan drowning in the pool.

She had been three when her brother died, and she'd dreamed it ever since. She still remembered sitting on the porch with her Dad and asking him if Dylan was in the moon and hearing his sure adult voice answer yes. She had been wearing some white sun dress with yellow boats floating on the skirt that her mom had made for her. Gabi talked to the moon for years, knowing that

Dylan had a better perspective on all the things that bothered her. She couldn't talk to anyone about her feelings, since the family seemed to have an unspoken agreement to never talk about Dylan and the events of that year.

Gabi went to her night classes in a group, but her imagination amazed her. Every bush, tree, classroom chair and desk had sinister underpinnings. So many of the students, especially freshmen, had gone home. Even Gabi's upper-division classes were half empty. Little carts buzzed around campus delivering female students to their dorms or sorority houses. Gabi's worst moments were when she walked from her car in the lot, up the stairs to their apartment. Bryan had put double locks on the doors, and her dad had brought canisters of mace. He told them it was important that they conquer their fear, and then he went back to Tampa. The only way Gabi could explain how he was acting was that he was in shock because of her mom. She had felt safer than most of her friends because of Bryan, since the murderer attacked women who lived alone. But then last night, they had watched on television as police carried out the first male victim, a wrestler who shared an apartment and death with his woman friend.

This morning, Gabi had started crying when the man who sprayed for bugs rang the bell. She wouldn't let him in until the manager came, and she insisted that he stay until the man was gone. She had been leaving little signs for herself. She draped the cord from the blinds across the sliding glass doors, checking to see if it was in the same place when she came home. She put small pieces of paper between the front door and the jamb and looked for them on the ground before she put her key in the lock.

Gabi thought about her dad's explanation for having their grandmother come to stay. He said to have activity around the place all day would discourage anything weird. He didn't understand what it was like. Four girls who were living alone had moved into the apartment. They slept on couches or on the floor. Everybody was scared to death. Phil Donahue did his show from downtown, and Gainesville was on the front page of every paper in the State. Gabi thought the Donahue thing was sick and wrote a letter in the student newspaper protesting his appearance.

She was sure her mom hadn't been told what was going on. Her dad said she had really lost it, going to Oregon to do some kind of New Age getting in touch with her inner self kind of thing. The letter she wrote to Gabi before she left said she was going to visit Aunt Lisa and then they were going to some kind of seminar. Gabi hated to admit she hadn't read the letter very carefully. Her mom had sent cookies, and she and Bryan had given the letter a quick once-over and then gorged on chocolate chips and pecans before their friends came. Gabi didn't think that baking cookies was something someone would do who was about to go off the deep end. She remembered her mom's letter as sounding cheerful. Her dad did say they were sure it wasn't a suicide attempt. He seemed more angry that she had decided to stay with those people in Oregon until she recovered, even though one of them had saved her life. Gabi thought he was just more scared than anything. She'd tried to call, but the hospital said there were no phones in the place they had her mom. Then Aunt Lisa told her it was because of the breathing tubes, but those were coming out soon. She was counting on her grandmother to shed some light.

Gabi looked out the window and saw her grandmother getting off the plane in the rinky-dink airport like the Queen of England.

"Remember," she reminded herself, "it's Eleanor, not Grandmother, Eleanor, not Grandmother." Gabi smiled. She really admired her grandmother. Maureen had told Gabi how Eleanor had remade her life when Grandpa died. Gabi never knew her grandfather, but he sounded like a tough cookie. Her mom usually changed the subject when he came up. But Eleanor had a new life, and looking and acting like a grandmother had no place in it.

The pilot himself escorted Eleanor down the steps and across the field, carrying her Gucci luggage. Gabi grinned and ran out on the concrete pad, then slowed down, remembering how her grandmother disliked what she called unladylike behavior. She reached out her hands, surprised to feel those easy tears coming again.

"Gabrielle! How lovely you look." Eleanor turned her around, and she blushed bright red as the pilot watched. "You're a grown woman. Tall and slender like your father. How fortunate you were to get his genes."

Gabi leaned over and brushed her grandmother's cheek with her lips. She had her usual sense of some kind of slight to her mother that she could never put her finger on.

"Hi, Grandma. I mean, Eleanor." She backed away at the look of displeasure on her grandmother's face. "I'm sorry. It takes a little time for me to get back in the habit."

Eleanor smiled and patted her arm. "We have plenty of time dear." She introduced Gabi to the pilot, Captain something-or-other. In the small waiting area, he put Eleanor's suitcase down and touched the bill of his cap. "Good luck in college," he said, smiling, and walked off.

"Oh, don't look so shocked, Gabrielle. He was just joking. Though I may look into auditing a couple of courses. I never did go past high school, and there are lots of things that interest me."

"So I see," Gabi teased, looking at the pilot's back as he walked away. She picked up the suitcase.

"How's Mom?" she asked, putting the luggage in the trunk.

"Aren't we going to pick up the rest of my things, Gabrielle?"

"I thought this was it."

"The nice man was just helping me with my carry-on. You don't think I could exist for a month with only one suitcase, do you?"

"A month?" Gabi's voice sounded unnaturally loud in the humid air.

"Well, who knows? Until they get this horrible man or your father comes to his senses and brings you home, whichever comes first."

Gabi switched on the air conditioning. "You can wait here, and I'll go get your things." She nearly leapt from the car. A month or whatever? They hoped the murderer would be caught any minute.

Gabi shoved the last piece of luggage in and slammed the trunk closed. She drove west toward her apartment complex. She hoped Bryan had finished cleaning up the remains of last night's pepperoni pizza and chicken wings still laying in their cardboard.

"Tell me about Mom. What's happening?"

Eleanor sighed. "I really don't understand any of it, Gabrielle."

Gabi looked sideways at her grandmother. The afternoon sun revealed her age under the carefully applied makeup. Gabi felt a twinge of sadness and put her hand over her grandmother's.

"I don't know where to start. As you know, we were called to Portland when your mother had her," she paused, "her accident. It was touch and go for awhile."

"What do you mean, touch and go? When Dad called us, he said she was doing fine."

"Well, your father was just trying to save you from worrying. Maybe he was trying to reassure himself too. Your mother was unconscious for two days. She has multiple broken bones and bruises. They put bolts in her ankle. Can you imagine that? Bolts?" Eleanor shuddered. "The doctors say it will take time. It was a miracle she wasn't killed."

Gabi swerved around another car, shaking her head at the blare of its horn. "I can't believe this. Why didn't you tell us? We should have been there."

"Gabrielle, dear, you had just left for school. You were beginning classes. What earthly good would it have done for you to be there? Your father was only thinking of your welfare."

"But what about Mom? Maybe she needed us." Gabi slowed as they passed the university administration building, and Eleanor rolled down her window. She quickly rolled it up again.

"This heat is unbearable," she gasped. Sweat was breaking through her makeup. She took out a handkerchief and dabbed at her face. "Your mother will be fine. What she needs is to know you're doing all right. As for this murder business, we won't tell her any of that. She knows I've come to visit you to explain everything about her accident. That should be enough."

Grandma and Dad, Gabi thought, always arranging things. She wondered how her mother had felt about that and felt a sudden sympathy.

"Did Mom say anything before you left?"

"As a matter of fact, they had just taken out her breathing tube …"

"Aunt Lisa said that's why she couldn't call us," Gabi interrupted. "Can she call us now?"

"In a day or so, Gabrielle. When her voice gets stronger. For now, you need to keep your mind on your school so you can make your parents proud of you."

Gabi kept her mouth shut. She knew it must have been really hard on her grandmother, worrying about her daughter, having to fly to Oregon and then back here. She would need to be more patient, like Bryan. She pulled into the parking lot at the apartment complex. "Well, here we are."

Eleanor looked up at the faux brick building and forced a smile. " I'm sure we'll be fine, dear. It will just take a little adjusting." A real smile broke over her face as she saw Bryan loping down the stairs, his brown hair bouncing on his neck, his dimple in full force.

"Hi grand … Eleanor," he said, stooping to hug her. "Gosh, you're as small as a kid in grade school. We'll have to fatten her up a little, huh Gabi?"

Gabi laughed at him. "After we take in her luggage. Maybe she'd like some chicken wings."

Eleanor turned pale. "Tonight I'll take you out for dinner. Tomorrow we'll go to the store."

Bryan's face lit up. "Groceries. I can't wait." He took the stairs two at a time, luggage under both arms and swinging from his hands.

"He's a wonder, Gabrielle. So full of life, even in this heat."

Gabi heard the sadness in her grandmother's voice.

She saw the apartment through her grandmother's eyes, a woman who lived in a condominium and spent most of her time in luxury suites on cruise ships. She really cared to have come here.

She took Eleanor's arm, and they went up the flight of stairs together.

"He's right, you know. You could use a little fattening up." At the top, Eleanor stopped and caught her breath. The small, perfectly manicured hands she held to her chest were so childlike that Gabi suddenly felt protective. Her grandmother stepped gingerly across the threshold like she was going into a bird cage. Bryan stood there beaming, his pride in the small space carpeted in gold shag and the thrift store Danish modern furniture as great as that of a duke welcoming guests to his castle.

Gabi slid in behind her grandmother, her lips twitching. "Show Eleanor her room, Bryan. I'll get us some lunch."

In the kitchen, she opened the cupboard, thoughts of her mom flooding over her. Was her grandmother right? Was her mom better off in Oregon than here with them? Gabi sighed as she opened a can of tuna. Good thing it was a weekend. The girls who stayed with them wouldn't be over until later. It would give her grandmother time to adjust. She heard the television go on in the other room, recognizing the droning voice of the sheriff. It was a daily occurrence, this recapping of the murders, reassuring everyone with pictures of the National Guard downtown along with police from other counties. This morning some newsman had said he figured the guy was long gone, probably in California or Mexico by now.

Gabi was surprised to notice that she felt better with her grandmother in the next room. It was like it used to be with Mom. Gabi was stronger and younger, but having her mom around had always made her feel protected. She blinked to keep the tears out of the tuna fish as she thought of Maureen. She must have been so scared. Gabi wished for the hundredth time that she was with her, but she knew Eleanor was right. If she left school and went to be with her mom, everyone would just worry, and she would create more problems. And there was Bryan to think about.

She wiped her eyes and put the sandwiches and chips on paper plates. She never cried. Where was this coming from? She carried lunch into the small dining area where her grandmother and Bryan were looking at the television. Bryan turned to her, his sparkling hazel eyes dulled to grey. "There's been another one, Gabi."

Eleanor was as pale as bleached out summer grass. Gabi reached for her as the harsh ring of the phone covered the voice on TV. Like a sleepwalker, Gabi picked it up.

"Hello? Hello? Gabi? Are you there? It's dad."

Gabi started to cry and couldn't stop. She handed the phone to her grandmother. On the couch next to Bryan, she kept crying, old tears she'd kept at bay for so long. Bryan put his arm around her and rubbed her shoulder over and over, brushing his own eyes with his other hand. The murmur of Eleanor's voice on the phone filled the background. By the time they finished their conversation, Gabi had gotten herself under control.

"God, I'm sorry. I've been so cool and then 'bam,' all of the sudden a basket case."

"You're like your mother, Gabrielle. You hold things in too long, in my opinion." She patted Gabi awkwardly on the head. "Tears are a woman's best weapon, my dear granddaughter. You should let them work for you." She cleared her throat. "Your father is coming tomorrow morning. He has something to tell you, and he wants to talk about what's next."

"What do you mean, what's next?" Bryan asked.

"It's obviously time to reconsider staying here."

Bryan straightened, his hand on Gabi's shoulder clenching.

"Well," Eleanor said, her hands on her hips, "I'm not going to be of any use in an emergency, now am I? This sick pervert is obviously not gone." Her head turned toward the television. News people were gathered in front of a familiar looking apartment complex.

"God, Gabi." Bryan gripped her hand. "That's just down the street. Isn't that where your friend, Bett, lives?"

The chain rattled on the door as someone pounded to get in. It was some of the overnight group, Bett in the middle of them. Gabi took a deep breath of relief and let them in.

"Who are these people, Bryan?" Eleanor whispered, as Gabi hugged the girls one at a time.

"They're our overnighters. They keep sleeping bags and stuff here. It makes them more comfortable to sleep in a group."

"It's only midafternoon." Eleanor looked at her watch.

"I guess they heard the news and decided to come early. They'll be using this floor once we go to bed tonight."

"Something which I intend to do right this minute, Bryan. I'm in dire need of a nap," Eleanor replied and went sailing off to the upstairs bedroom with her sandwich in her hand. She turned at the head of the stairs. "Don't forget, your father will be here in the morning. Try to keep things orderly." She swept a look around the group below and turned her back. "We'll eat out," floated behind her.

Jason arrived early the next morning. The four of them went to Skeeters Restaurant. They were seated after an hour long wait. It was like a football weekend without the festivity. Parents hovered over their kids, talking fervently. Decisions were being made that would change lives forever. The blue grass group that had been on since five in the morning was finally taking a break, and Eleanor discreetly removed her hands from over her ears. The restaurant prided itself on twenty-four hours a day of music and food. There were always budding musicians ready to comply in the wee hours. Jason looked like he'd been on the road all night, even though the drive from Tampa was more like two hours. He guzzled his first cup of coffee, held it out for a refill, and then gave his attention to the menu. Eleanor looked at the trays of eggs and cheese grits passing by, the big-as-a-plate biscuits crowned with sausage gravy.

"Where's the no-fat menu?" she whispered to Bryan.

"Not here," he replied. "There's a twenty-four hour buffet, though. It has Chinese food and ribs and stuff on it." Eleanor paled. "Just orange juice and dry toast, please," she instructed the waitress.

Jason ordered poached eggs and toast. The waitress said she'd ask the kitchen if they could poach them. He looked from the waitress to Gabi for the first time, and she felt an unfamiliar empathy as she saw the dark rings under his eyes. He usually seemed so remote and self-assured.

Jason fiddled with his napkin, tearing the paper into strips. "I guess we need to make some decisions here, but I can't for the life of me figure out what to do. It seems to me you both need to come home. Just call this a lost semester and start over when this is finished."

"But Dad," Bryan pleaded. "We're being really careful, and with Eleanor here …" His voice trailed off. "I know what you're saying. If we hadn't put in so much time, I wouldn't care, but we could get killed driving back to Tampa just as easily!"

"Bryan, I've been over all of this in my mind, and I said the same thing. Still, you don't intentionally put yourself or your sister in harm's way." Jason sighed. "Besides," he said, his voice barely audible, "your mother would never forgive me."

"She doesn't know any of this, does she?" Gabi asked.

Jason shook his head. "But with this latest one, it's gone national, and she's going to find out. They moved her this morning to that Emania place."

He nearly choked on the word. "There's no television there, believe it or not, but someone's bound to talk about it. And I can't deal with it anymore. I've got work to do. They gave a big case to another attorney when I had to fly to Oregon during the pretrial hearings. Where would this family be if I didn't work? You need to come home for now, and that's all there is to it." He stopped, gasping, the whole speech having been delivered in one breath.

Gabi and Bryan stared, neither daring a word.

Eleanor patted his hand. "We all know how hard you work, dear. If the children can come home and be helping you at the same time, I'm sure they'll do the right thing."

"What kind of help are you talking about, Dad?" Gabi asked.

"I'm not asking for help. Of course, with your mother gone," he paused, gathering himself again just as the fiddle players tuned for the next set. He raised his voice. "Your mother has only worked off and on," he began, triggering pictures in Gabi's mind of her mother bent over the ironing board, the stove, the baby's crib, "but I counted on her to keep the house running in some semblance of order. The bills are behind, the house is ..." He shook his head and cleared his throat. "And she's not coming back. She's asked for a divorce."

Into the deathly silence of their table, the fiddles returned, swinging into a spirited Irish jig. Jason pushed his plate to the side, dropped two twenties on the table and nearly ran out the door. Eleanor followed him, leaving Gabi and Bryan staring at each other.

Finally, Gabi spoke. "Mom did too work," she said and got up to follow her father. They waited in the car for ten minutes before Bryan joined them, his eyes red and his fair skin splotchy around his mouth.

By late afternoon, it was settled. Jason would leave tonight, taking Eleanor with him to Tampa. Gabi and Bryan would withdraw from school in the morning, pack up and come home on Tuesday. The overnighters had fanned out, looking for other places to stay, and Eleanor was taking a short nap when Bryan found Gabi crying on the back steps facing the parking lot.

"It's not the worst thing in the world, Gabi. We can come back as soon as this guy is in jail."

Gabi wiped her eyes on her sleeve. "Did you ever think that Mom and Dad would get divorced, Bryan?" She looked over at him. "Ever?"

Bryan sat down on the step below her. "C'mon, Gabi. It happens to lots of people. Mom and Dad have been trying to work this thing out for a long time. Maybe it's time they gave it up."

"How can you say that? Sure, they had problems, but . . ." She looked up and saw the moisture glint in Bryan's eyes.

"Maybe they just came together to make us and now they have other things to do," he said quietly, his words hanging in the humid air.

"Sure, right." She wrapped her arms around her legs, waiting for him to go on, say he was just joking, but he didn't. "You're serious, aren't you? You really believe there's a reason for everything."

He looked at her, his eyes clear as rainbows against a dark sky. "Don't you?"

"Then what about Dylan?" She held her breath, counted the sweat drops sliding between her shoulder blades. She'd gone too far to turn back. She and Bryan had never said their brother's name out loud.

Bryan looked up at her, and she was struck with such love for the goodness of the soul that looked out of his eyes. "I've thought about that almost all my life. Why him? I never knew him like you did, but I *feel* like I did. I was born on the day he was buried. Do you know what that feels like? Mom trying to act like it was a day to celebrate, and all the time . . . It's really hard to explain."

Gabi watched the clouds pile up in the west as Bryan struggled to put his thoughts into words. She pictured him as a baby, so serious and quiet that they called him "The Thinker." And he'd always talked them out of throwing a party on his birthday, saying he'd rather just be with family.

"I have to believe there's a reason. Maybe it was to send each of us off on our own path, something that wouldn't have happened if we had lived happily ever after. I'm still not sure what that path means for me, but I'll know when the time comes."

Gabi rubbed his head with her hand. She wished, not for the first time, that she had Bryan's sureness. "How did you get so smart, little brother?"

"Dylan's death was a needless tragedy," Eleanor said from the landing behind them. "How can you think there was a reason for such a terrible thing? If your mother hadn't gone back to school, he wouldn't have been riding that bus all alone, little tyke that he was." Her words hung over the group like poison gas.

"Eleanor, you promised you would never say that again as long as you lived." Jason's voice came from below. None of them had heard him drive up.

"I don't know why I did," Eleanor cried, tears clogging her voice. "It's just this horrible atmosphere … all the death and sadness. It's bringing it all back. That's why these children need to come home and Maureen needs to be there, where she belongs."

"We're not children, Grandmother, and Mom was always there. I hope you never said any of that to her." Bryan was on his feet, his usually soft voice clear and cold like snow in February.

"How dare you use that tone with me? I'm not a child to be chastised. And she wasn't there, at least not that time … and she knows it."

Jason came up the last flight of stairs. "Bryan, bring your grandmother's suitcases. We need to start before dark." Jason put an arm around Gabi. "We'll get through this somehow. Together, OK?"

Minutes later, Bryan wedged the last suitcase in Jason's trunk and stepped away, his face closed up tight. He held the door for his grandmother, staying far enough away to avoid any contact.

Gabi stood still on the steps, watching her father, her grandmother and Bryan like a dream in slow motion. Bryan's face reminded her of a book she had read years ago where a fundamentalist father shunned his son for the remainder of his life for some sin she couldn't remember. When the car pulled away, she thought about raising her hand to wave, but it was too much effort. She heard Bryan tell her he was going for a walk, and she thought she might have nodded her assent. When he got back, she was still sitting there, her clothes wet from a brief afternoon shower that provided no relief from the heat. Bryan put his hand under her elbow and helped her inside.

"We'll manage this, Sis. It's OK. We'll talk to Mom when she gets home," his voice choked. "No wonder she went off like she did. Do you think they've always blamed her?"

Gabi couldn't answer him. "I need to take a nap. All of this is … I don't know," she finished in a whisper.

Bryan looked closely at his sister as she headed for the couch. "You don't look so good. We didn't get any breakfast or lunch now that I think about it, with Dad jumping up like he did. Let me fix you something."

Gabi waved her hand at him. "Maybe later …"

"At least change your clothes. You're all wet."

"In a minute." Gabi sat on the couch, carefully as if her bones hurt. "You know what? When I get up, I'm calling Aunt Lisa."

Bryan let his breath out. "That's a great idea. She'll be straight with us." He looked at his watch. "I'm going to go get us something to eat. No sense in buying groceries now." Bryan turned at the door. "Will you be OK?" Gabi nodded, her eyes closed. "Just lock the door after you," she whispered, sleep already overtaking her.

Bryan watched her for a minute. He wondered if she knew how much she looked like their Mom. He locked and chained the front door and let himself out through the kitchen, thinking with relief of calling Aunt Lisa. She was so practical. He didn't notice the bicycle propped behind the dumpster or the man sitting next to it, watching, as Bryan backed out in the Honda.

Chapter Ten

Gabi heard the voice in a dream, and even when she felt the sharp point prick her neck and a trickle of her own blood slide down over her collar bone, she tried to believe she was still dreaming. The voice, whispery and coated with the odor of stale beer, ordered her to keep her eyes closed. She couldn't have opened them in any case. All of her body was caught in that frozen state suffered in the worst nightmares. Even her brain's order to inhale didn't register until she gasped and her chest lifted slightly.

"I know your boyfriend's gone, darlin', so just relax, and you and me are gonna have a little party."

Gabi heard the rip before she felt her blouse tear away. He held his fist against her throat, letting just enough air through for her to stay conscious. With the knife, he cut through the front of her bra, and she felt the air caress her freed breasts with cruel gentleness. Now she was awake, fully awake to the reality of the nightmare, but she kept her eyes closed. She knew absolutely that if she saw him, saw the face of this person, she would not survive. She struggled to free her legs from an enormous weight pinning her into the cushions of the couch.

"I said don't move, sweetheart," he said, his voice calm and reasonable, like her third grade teacher, Mr. Johnson. Then he slammed his fist into her cheek.

She felt a sickening sense of her face caving in, its shape altered forever into this man's choosing. She tried to picture Dylan in her mind, but this time, she saw only the moon, dark and shadowed. Her arms were trapped beneath his torso, and she was losing feeling in her legs. The body pressing down on her was heavy as wet earth except for the twitching penis she could feel hardening on her stomach. Bile rose in her throat, burning, and she felt she would choke to death. Blood filled her nose and the pain from her cheek screamed up into her ear. He fumbled at his zipper, little groans escaping from his mouth, his breath stifling in the close air. Her mind escaped her body, seemed to sit on a chair across the room, watching, waiting for the afternoon thunderstorm to cut the air, the lightning to strike right down the middle of him. She pictured his head exploding as she watched him shove her legs apart with his knee and ram himself into her dry, fleeing, womanhood. She heard his grunt and then a woman's voice, high and wailing, pierced through her. For just a moment the knife slid from her neck, resting quietly on her shoulder, and she was back in her body.

"Tight cunt," he mumbled, just as she heard the crash of thunder, felt his body shudder and become lax, felt the blood trickle down the inside of her thighs and the pain stab deep inside her. She would die now, she thought, as she waited for him to finish his work.

*****

"Gabi, open your eyes! Please. Gabi, Please." Bryan's voice was the sound of a broken-hearted child. His tears dropped on her face stinging in the open wound like the waters of the Gulf of Mexico.

She opened the one eye she could manage and saw Bryan kneeling next to the couch. She could hear the rain pelting the roof. The weight was gone. "Where?" Her voice cracked.

He held up a tire iron. "You don't have to be afraid. I tied him up. The police and the ambulance are coming. Hold on, Sis." His voice broke as he laid a gentle hand on her hair. She noticed she was covered with a blanket and there was a wet cloth on one side of her face.

"I'm so sorry, Sis. I shouldn't have gone and left you here." The anguish in his voice was palpable, like a small animal in a trap. She tried to lift a hand, to stop him from taking responsibility for this, but she couldn't. So much guilt. This family was dying of it. She smelled onions and hamburgers. Her stomach roiled.

"I was parking the car ..." Bryan took a deep shuddering breath. "I saw the sliding door open. I grabbed the tire iron out of the back of the car. When I came in," he choked. "When I came in ..." There was a long silence. "He didn't even hear me."

The door banged open, and the room filled with people in uniforms. The ones in white bent over Gabi, and she felt herself slip away, gratefully, to a quiet, grey place.

The doctors couldn't explain Gabi's condition. They compared it to post traumatic stress, but even that didn't fit. She wasn't in a coma, but she wasn't in the world. It was as if she had called timeout and just gone somewhere else. Bryan seemed to be the only one who wasn't afraid for her. As Maureen and Jason sat in ICU by her bed, he told them she would come back when she was ready. Meanwhile, plans went ahead for the reconstructive surgery on her face. The rest of her wounds were of a different sort. Maureen sat by the bed in a wheel chair with her leg elevated in its cast. After Gabi's first surgery, Jason went back to Tampa, and they gave Maureen a room of her own just down the hall.

The trip from California had transpired in a haze of pain killers and recriminations. Even as she got on the plane and Stephen was tucking her into the bulkhead seat, she was shaking her head in denial of him.

"It *is* my fault. When I'm not there, things happen. I'm supposed to be there. I promised."

*****

When Stephen walked out of the airport, people gave him space, walked ten feet out of their way to avoid his path. He looked like a man who had barely survived a war and wished he hadn't. Brigit had waited for him in the station wagon, and her heart broke for him as he walked slowly toward her, his arm was still in a cast, and the bruises from the accident were turning the garish yellow-blue that meant he was healing. She felt his misery like dense fog inside the car as they drove silently back to Emania. Stephen had been in Portland helping Maureen with her physical therapy for the past two weeks, and their joy at being together was part of the reason for their rapid recovery. The doctors had been stunned at the relatively minor injuries, outside of the broken bones, the two had sustained. They had laughed together as he, one-armed, tried to help her, one-legged, on their daily walks through the hospital halls. And then came the phone call from Lisa, and it had all ended as quickly as it started.

"Stephen, she'll be back. I know it. She knows she's meant to be with you."

"You don't know, Brigit. Her guilt over Dylan, now over Gabi." He shook his head again, and she knew he had given up. "Once she's back in Tampa, all the old habits and beliefs are going to be stronger than anything that happened here."

"Even stronger than love? Stephen, she loves you with all her heart."

"But she loves her children. Which would you choose?" he asked, looking at her for the first time.

"They're not children anymore, Stephen. You're talking like Maureen now."

"I'm thinking like her. That's the only way I can convince myself of what I know she'll do. Did you know her mother blamed her when Dylan died?"

"That's impossible."

"She decided to go back to school when Dylan entered first grade. She let him ride the bus so she could get Gabi ready for the babysitter and have dinner ready. In Eleanor's eyes, she should have been content to take care of the kids, like her mother was."

"You knew them back then, Stephen. What kind of mother was Eleanor?"

"On again, off again, I guess. When she wasn't fighting with her husband or depressed because he was cheating on her, she smothered them with direction. In her memory, though, she was always there." He laughed, a harsh sound so unlike him that Brigit was frightened. "She credits her sacrifices for them turning out so well." He looked out the window, watching the shadow of a huge plane fly across the field and disappear. "What's the point? Maureen's sense of who she is came from them for so long. Do you really think a weekend at Emania can change all that?"

"Of course not, not without work. But your love *has* to change all that."

"You read too much romance, Brigit," he shot back, then covered her hand on the wheel with his. "I'm sorry. I know what you're saying," he smiled slightly, "and I know you don't read romances. It's just that I know them. They're stronger than her."

"Well, maybe it's time you gave Maureen a little credit."

"Do you know what she's going to find when she gets there? Her daughter has gone off-planet, raped and battered, her son taking the blame for not being there, her husband and mother blaming her for taking time for herself when the kids were in jeopardy."

"C'mon Stephen. She didn't even *know* about the murders in Gainesville. If anyone's to blame for them not coming home, its Jason."

"That's exactly why he'll convince her it's her fault. He can't accept the blame." He shook his head. "No. For her to think of herself, let alone me, at a time like this would be a sacrilege to her." He slumped against the door. "And I can't imagine going back to life without her. Maybe I'm as bad as they are. We're all so needy!"

"It's different, Stephen. She needs you, too. You belong together."

He didn't answer, and they made the rest of the trip in silence, his pain a living presence filling the car.

*****

In Gainesville, Maureen leaned on her crutches, watching the rain run down the waiting room's one window. Her leg throbbed from the damp air, and she smothered a sob. Jason got up and came to her, his hand tentative on her back.

"She's going to be fine. The doctor said she'd be just like new. You heard him." He raised his voice slightly. "Maureen?"

"Like new," she whispered. She leaned her forehead on the chilled glass pane. How easy she had thought that was, just a short time ago. Maybe the silicone cheek implant and the tiny internal sutures of the careful surgeons would make Gabi's face hers again, but for the rest of it? Maureen shivered. That monster had stolen something far more important. Funny, sensible, Gabi was gone, and a blank stranger was in her place looking out through Gabi's eyes.

"C'mon, Maureen. Sit down and rest. You can't do her any good like this." Jason's voice verged on the edge of panic.

She knew what he was thinking, what he was always thinking. He'd built such a careful life, one that denied all the messiness of his parents' existence. He was sure to wonder how all this happened to him. Chaos was only for other people. She saw his face lighten.

"You're home now," he said. "Things will be all right." He looked at her questioningly. She knew what he was asking. Was the divorce off?

She felt the blackness around her get darker. Yes, she was home now. Jason coughed as the family at the other end of the waiting room lit up their cigarettes. Maureen touched his wrist as he started to go down and remind them that this was a nonsmoking facility.

"Don't, Jason. We can go somewhere else. They're here for the boy in the bed next to Gabi," she whispered. "The doctors are saying there's no hope."

"How do you know these things? I've been waiting here in the same room as you. OK. I won't say anything. Damn, sometimes I wished I still smoked." A small smile twitched at his mouth. "Remember when Gabi and Bryan hid my cigarettes, and I got so mad? Gabi brought home that black lung from her science class—smuggled it right out of there."

Maureen smiled back at the memory. "And you had to sit and listen while she gave you the whole lecture about dying tissues and strangling oxygen, complete with Bryan's sound effects." She stopped.

"He was especially effective with the strangling oxygen," Jason said. "Let's go find a quiet place with clean air."

The volunteer lady in the pink dress pointed them to a room down the hall. "I'll tell the doctors where to find you when the surgery's over."

The door was marked with a small discreet sign that said "Contemplation Room." Inside, a stained glass window hung over a marble ledge. No statues or incense, no kneelers for penitents, no holy water. Just a quiet blue room with benches and the stained glass of no discernible pattern.

Like life, Maureen thought. Just random strikes of good or bad. She felt Jason guide her onto the padded bench, the pain in her leg a throbbing reminder. No, that wasn't true, the random part. Bad things happened when she wasn't careful. She had forgotten about vigilance. An image of Stephen floated in front of the stained glass, and she banished him. There was the danger. She had forfeited him when she promised Jason "in sickness and in health, until death ..." and gave birth to their children. How could she have forgotten? She closed her eyes, stretching the leg in front of her that throbbed like a heart trying to break through the splintered bones. She fumbled in her purse for a pain pill.

"I'll go get some water," Jason said, glad to have something concrete to do. Maureen sat and tried to conjure up the face of Jesus, his mother or even St. Joseph, the one who made the triangle of the family complete. Nothing came. Only the picture of Gabi's blank eyes sunken in black circles over the bandages, a picture that she couldn't get out of her mind.

At first, they had thought Gabi's attacker was the murderer, but he had an alibi for every one of them. Every day since had been a small step to today. The doctors had removed blood clots and bone splinters, set her nose and then treated her for the fever that followed. She would have to have dental work later, but today was the major surgery, replacing the bone in her cheek with bone taken from her ribs. Maureen felt the pain working up into her hip. Where was Jason?

The door opened and three women and a man came in. They knelt together on the floor, holding hands and began praying aloud. First one, then another, prayed for Robert, the boy in ICU. Maureen felt the tears slide from under her lids at the fervent prayers for the young man who lay so blue and quiet on the ice bed. She sensed the man standing in front of her, a faint odor of rain and coffee emanating from him.

"Let us pray with you. Is it your lovely daughter we see when we visit our boy?"

Maureen nodded.

"We heard what happened. She has our love and the Lord's love. Hold our hands in the circle of Jesus, sister, and all will be as it's meant to be." His damp hand clung to hers as the prayers became louder and more fervent. On her other side, the tiny bird-like hand of an older woman fluttered in hers.

"Pray, sister," the man urged, squeezing her hand hard. "All must be together and righteous before blessings will flow."

She heard the words "miracle" and "blessing" time after time as she tried to concentrate, tried to believe that these prayers would rise to the throne of God and be answered. She was dizzy with pain and effort. Where was Jason? Then, through the pain, she heard the words "if even one here has doubt, our prayers will not rise." She jerked her hand away. No. She would not be responsible for what happened to that boy. How could they ask this of her? She didn't believe. Couldn't believe. She had to move. She heaved herself onto her crutches and slid toward the door just as Jason approached, and then the pain took over.

Hours later the doctor came in the waiting room, the smile on his face enough to bring Maureen to her feet. Jason held her elbow in a tight grip.

"She came through like a trooper. Barring unforseen complications, you won't be able to tell there was a surgery. Light makeup will cover any scarring."

"What kind of complications?" Jason asked.

The smile faded from the surgeons face. "In surgical cases, the patient's attitude is crucial to recovery, and we haven't been able to get through to Gabi. Is there anyone you know who could talk to her? Sometimes, in cases like hers, a male figure in her life can convince her that she's still …" he hesitated.

"Still what?" Jason asked.

"Well, desirable. You know, that it's not her fault, that she *will* be herself again."

Maureen thought of Gabi's "on again, off again" boyfriend, Robert, who had called after they got to Gainesville and said he just couldn't handle it. And he hadn't. She shook her head. "I can't believe this sort of assault could lead to the kind of things you're talking about. I know some women are told it was their fault because of the way they dressed or whatever. I just don't see the reasoning here. She was at home." Maureen started to shake. "She was taking a nap." Her voice broke. Jason's hand tightened on her arm.

"Calm down, Maureen. That isn't what the doctor said. We're looking for a counselor and a support group for Gabrielle back in Tampa, doctor. In the meantime, her family will be here."

"Both of those will be helpful, Mr. Manley," the doctor said, concentrating on him with relief. "She'll be here another week if nothing develops. Then the real work starts." He shook hands with Jason. "I wish you luck." As he left the room, Maureen saw flecks of blood on the green booties over his shoes. She sat heavily.

Jason let out a sigh. "I have to go home tonight. Will you be OK?"

Maureen nodded. "Bryan's on his way up. We'll stay at a hotel." She raised her cheek for his kiss. "Drive carefully," she said, then rested her head on the plastic seat back.

Jason pulled a stool up for her leg. "I hate to leave you like this, but there's nothing I can do here, and I have a case going."

Maureen waved her hand at him, her speech slurring as if she'd been drinking, the sudden fatigue like a tent descending over her. "I'm just going to sleep. Bryan should be here any minute. Go. Please." Her eyes closed, and she heard his footsteps fade down the hall, picking up speed as he neared the door. Bryan would be the key, she thought, speeding toward sleep. She closed her eyes. If he could face it. She fell asleep with the faces of her children hanging on her dreams like talismans.

*****

"Mom?" Bryan patted her shoulder. "Gabi's awake. We can go in now."

Maureen struggled out of her dream and stood, Bryan's strong arm supporting her. "How long have you been here?" she asked, her mouth so dry she had trouble forming the words.

"A couple of hours. I ran into Dad in the parking lot. I saw Gabi's doctor in the hall, and I told him I'd help. She's going to be OK, Mom. We'll all be OK."

For a moment, Maureen didn't trust herself to speak. She pointed to the restroom, and Bryan helped her to the door. She washed her face, fluffing her hair with stiff fingers. She saw her face in the mirror and was repelled by what she saw; pasty white skin splotched with old bruises uncovered by makeup, eyes red rimmed from pain and lack of sleep. She looked like she'd been beaten. She fished in her purse for a compact and lipstick. She ran a brush through her hair which had grown out to nearly its old length and lay lusterless against her neck. She went out to where Bryan waited impatiently.

"They only give us ten minutes, Mom."

"That's enough for today, Bryan. I didn't want Gabi worrying about me on top of everything else."

In the anteroom, they washed with sterile soap and donned masks and gowns. Maureen staggered slightly as they neared the bed where machines beeped and gurgled and wove their way in and out of her child's body. The only parts recognizable as Gabi were the freckles sprinkling her forehead and the lanky length of her under the sheet. Her dark hair with its sheen of red was a dull brown where it curled out under the bandages, and her quick hazel eyes were hidden behind purpled eyelids.

Bryan took one hand and Maureen the fingers of the other, gently, below the needle taped to the back of her hand. Blue showed through Gabi's white skin, skin she nursed out of the sun as the brown goddesses of Florida romped on the beaches.

"Gabi, it's Mom and Bryan. We're here if you need us. The surgery went well. Your doctor is pleased." She stopped, the visiting hour words stuck in her throat.

Gabi's eyelids flicked open. She focused on her mom and then turned her gaze to Bryan. Her eyes turned from grey to blue-green, as if clouds had cleared from in front of the sun. If the rest of her face hadn't been covered with bandages, Maureen would have sworn she smiled.

A nurse came over. "We need to check her drain, Mrs. Manley. You can come back in the morning. Leave your number with the nurse at the desk."

Gabi's fingers gripped Maureen's. "What if she needs us?"

"We'll call, I promise," the nurse replied, her voice hurried. She looked down at Maureen's swollen leg. "*Both* of you need a good night's sleep," she said, her gentle hand on Maureen's shoulder belying the efficient tone. "Come after breakfast. I'll leave orders for you to be allowed to stay awhile."

Gabi looked in Maureen's eyes and blinked twice, then swung her eyes toward the door.

Maureen understood. "OK, honey. We'll see you in the morning."

On the way to the door, the stupefying fatigue overwhelmed her. Bryan drove them to the motel just down the street from Shands Hospital. After she was in the room, he left to get food.

"Lock the door, Mom, and don't let anyone in."

Maureen felt a warm flush through her cold body. It was good to be mothered. Then she shuddered. He must have told Gabi the same thing. When Bryan came back, she was bathed and dressed for bed.

"C'mon, Mom. Dad said you hadn't eaten today." He held out a chicken leg and a biscuit. "You need to take the advice you give to Gabi and me."

"OK, Bryan. But what about you?"

"I ate on the road," he mumbled, blushing.

She looked closely at her son, his usually vibrant being clouded, as if his spirit was wrapped in cobwebs. "You were right in what you said earlier, Bryan. We will get through this, but Gabi needs our help. She's been brutalized in her spirit as well as her body."

"I know." He sat on the edge of the bed. "When she went away, mentally? She was just trying to protect herself. She'll face all of it when she's strong enough. I know it."

Tears trembled on Maureen's lashes as she looked at her son, his distress written on his face like stigmata. She touched his hand. "She loves you so dearly. You'll be able to help her. I know that."

"But I should have protected her, Mom," he cried out. "I wasn't there."

"Oh, my God," Maureen whispered, the words echoing her own down the years. She prayed silently for the wisdom to say the right thing. "You saved her life. If it hadn't been for you ..." She shivered, unable to even think what might have happened. "We have a lot of forgiving to do in this family," she said, putting her arms around him. "Starting with ourselves."

"What do you have to forgive yourself for, Mom? You've done everything you could."

She heard her thoughts, her self saying "except to be there when you needed me" but she didn't say it aloud. Hadn't she just told him it wasn't his fault that he wasn't there? Which was true? Her head felt like bees were buzzing behind her eyes.

"Bryan, we just need to be realistic. We do our best and things happen, and we have to move on, one step at a time. Right now, step one is to rest and be strong for Gabi." She kissed his forehead and went to brush her teeth.

"OK, Mom. I'm going to watch the news."

Minutes later, Bryan banged on the bathroom door. "Mom! Come quick!"

She pushed herself through the door where Bryan stood staring at the television screen. Police surrounded a scar-faced boy, his hands cuffed behind him. The announcer was saying something about knives and the boy's grandmother being assaulted.

"They got him. They finally got him," Bryan whispered.

Maureen looked into the blank eyes of the boy facing the lights, his ill-fitting clothes looking like they belonged to someone else. "Maybe so," she said, but Bryan didn't hear her. She looked at the boy again as they put him in the police car. Where were the visible signs of evil, she wondered? Where was the brand that God should have provided as warning to those young people just beginning their lives and their families? She crawled into bed, the rattling room air conditioner blessedly drowning out the voice of the reporter.

Chapter Eleven

Gabi and Maureen sat on the patio in the early November sunshine snapping beans for supper. The bandages from Gabi's final surgery were off, and the bruises showed pale on her cheek, like shadows. Maureen still had a bandage over the screws in her ankle, but she rarely needed her crutches. Her leg was the family barometer, predicting rain hours before it arrived. She didn't tell them her head did the same.

"Mom?"

"Hmm?"

"Do you remember when you used to put me out here in the playpen while you worked in the yard?"

Maureen looked up, dropping the beans back into the bowl. "You were so small then." She touched her daughter's cheek, her hand damp and smelling like summer from the vegetables. "What do you remember?"

"Sitting in my playpen with the water sparkling on the pool. I remember staring at the water and then seeing you on your knees in the flower beds, shimmering color all around you. I can see my toys on the grass, and then they would fly through the air and land inside with me, and I would throw them out again. There was a ball, some squishy kind of doll, plastic keys on a chain." She looked at Maureen. "It was Dylan throwing them back in, wasn't it?"

Maureen nodded, her head back on the chair, her face raised to the sun. "He was four when we got the pool. He loved being responsible for you. He could stand there for hours just picking up what you threw out until you got tired of the game or I finished my work."

"I missed him so much, Mom. I thought for a while that you had traded him for Bryan, and I used to pray that God would trade them back."

Maureen cried out in pain.

"Mom? Are you OK? Is it your leg?"

"No, Gabi. My God, we are so self-centered. We thought if we just payed lots of attention, somehow you would get by. How could we have been so stupid? He was a huge part of your life." She sat, her hands still in the white bowl filled with green beans.

"Mom, you aren't in charge of the world. You had your own pain. I have a hard time remembering where Dad was then, except I remember asking him if Dylan was in the moon."

"You asked him that?"

"I did. And he told me yes, and I accepted his answer. I prayed to the moon until I was thirteen. I was only three, Mom. I'm sure I couldn't have told you what I was feeling if I knew myself. You did all you could." Gabi picked up a handful of beans. "I have some other memories that just pop out every once in awhile, usually like this one when we're doing something totally unrelated."

"Like what?"

"Oh, like when Grandma was babysitting, and Dylan would let me sleep in his room because I didn't like the way she snored."

"Eleanor snored?" Maureen sounded shocked. "She never did when I was in a room with her."

"Well, maybe she can control it. You know how she is about image." Gabi giggled.

Maureen looked at her, the sound filling her with joy. Gabi hadn't smiled in so long.

"I remember his blanket, too. The one with the ducks? I used to sit in the closet and hold it sometimes when you were gone."

"Oh, Gabi. Me too." Maureen was determined not to cry. Enough tears had been shed in this house. "What a pair."

"You know what else I remember? You reading to us. But my favorites were the stories you made up."

"Made up? I didn't make up stories, Gabi."

"Maybe not exactly. But you changed them around a lot."

"I didn't know you knew that."

"One of my first courses in Primary Ed was "kiddie lit." I recognized a lot of the stories, but there were always parts that were different."

"Like what?"

"Like where I thought the girl was the hero? Turned out it was always some prince or something."

"Well, I guess I did make them a little more … what do they call it now? Politically correct?"

Gabi laughed. "I guess you could say that."

"It's so beautiful out here," Maureen sighed, leaning forward. "Would you like to hear another story?" she asked, surprised at her own question.

"A story? Now?"

"This one I heard in Oregon, around the healing fire. It's about three sisters."

"Hold on a minute." Gabi went into the house, returning with two glasses of apple juice. She settled into the chaise with one, giving the other to her Mom. "OK. I'm ready."

"That's OK, Gabi. It was a silly idea."

"No, I want to hear."

Maureen leaned back in her chair and slowly and dramatically told her daughter the tale of Flamia, Gala, and the younger sister. She felt like she was initiating her daughter into a society she had only just joined.

When she finished, a communion between them vibrated in the living silence. A soft breeze blew through the yard, gently lifting the leaves. The season that made Florida worth living in had arrived. Together, they looked at the brilliant red blooms of the geraniums in clay pots against the dark green grass. Small puffy clouds dotted the clear sky, a sky so perfect it looked like Monet had painted it. And she felt the thoughts of her daughter joining with her and Dylan and all the ancestors before them. She began to remember Emania.

"Mom?"

"Yes, Gabi?"

"Today is the first day I've seen colors instead of grey. Thanks for the story. I'm not totally sure what it means, but I get a lot of it."

"Such as?"

"Well, we have to suffer before we appreciate what we have."

"Maybe so, Gabi." Maureen paused, thinking hard. "When I was in Oregon, I saw it as meaning no change was possible without deep introspection and pain and the companionship of women who have been where you have. I suppose your interpretation is more in line with the way I learned growing up." She laced her fingers together tightly. "And, I guess, the way I raised you. But it's deeper than that." She struggled for words. "It's like finding yourself when you think you're searching for something else." She shook her head in frustration. "Maybe that's why we have so many stories, because it's so hard to say it in normal words."

Gabi nodded. "I can relate to the sisters when I think about my group. They've saved my life. Maybe I can tell about Flamia and her sisters at the next meeting."

Maureen looked across to the bougainvillea blazing on the fence. "Sure you can. I'm really sorry, honey. I wish Brigit were here. She had such a clear way of seeing things. I guess you just have to find the meaning in it that's there for you."

"It seems like a good time. Since you mentioned Oregon, what happened to you out there? And who is Brigit?"

Maureen held the bowl from her lap and lifted awkwardly out of the chair. "Let's go inside and start dinner. I'll tell you about it while we cook. It's a very long story."

By the time the table was set, Maureen had finished telling Gabi about her time in Oregon with Lisa, up through the ceremony. She would never make the mistake again, if she could help it, of keeping everything locked up inside—of not letting people know who she really was. She didn't mention Stephen. In retelling the story of Brigit and the campfire, she'd felt a stirring inside, a reminder that something had happened to her, some changes had taken place. She had wrenched her old self back without destroying what had grown in its place, and she was too full, stuffed with things at war with one another. She sat at the dining room table while the bread heated. Jason would be home any minute. She looked down at the fresh tablecloth and saw a faint stain at the end. Something stung in her, some memory, and she felt the color drain from her face.

"Mom? Are you OK?" Gabi's voice traveled the long distance to where Maureen curled inside herself.

"Mom?"

"What? Yes. Yes, I'm fine." Maureen focused on her daughter. "My leg just hurts a little, that's all."

"No wonder with all you did today—working in the yard, cooking dinner. Dad's right. You need to take it easier."

"Gabi? Today was better for you, wasn't it?" She needed to be sure. It was important to know that her being here was resulting in Gabi's improvement.

"Every day I get a little better, but then … then there are really bad days." Gabi's eyes looked at a picture only she could see, then she shook herself, coming back to the room. "Going to my group is the most help. Mom, you wouldn't believe what some of those girls have been through. Only one of them still has a boyfriend, and some of them lost *all* of their friends."

"How do you feel about Robert, now that you've had some time to get used to him not being around?" Maureen asked, looking closely at Gabi.

"At first, I hated him. Then, for a while, I couldn't trust anyone. Then I just felt sorry for him, which is where I was yesterday. And then, out of the blue, he called."

"He called?"

"Last night." She sat down across from Maureen. "He's so intimidated by his parents. His mom came in the room, and he started whispering. Isn't that sad?"

Maureen watched Gabi's face. She was far off in thought. Then she shook her head as if to clear away the gloom.

"He wants to see me. He says he just needed time to get used to the idea, but now he knows it wasn't my fault."

"Your fault? He could have loved you and thought that?"

Gabi looked so sad Maureen's heart contracted. She reached across the table to her. "I'm sorry. I know that's so common, but I guess I react without logic because it's you. Are you going to see him?"

"I think so, Mom. We've been friends since fifth grade. And then, after our junior year, a lot more than friends. I've missed him a lot."

"Well, to tell the truth, once I got over being really pissed . . ."

Maureen laughed at Gabi's look of shock.

"Sorry, ticked off, at him, I started thinking about how much a part of the family he was. I'm glad he's come to his senses, but I don't think I'll ever feel the way I did before."

"Me neither, Mom, but I do want to see him. We have a lot to talk about."

Maureen's ears caught an odd sound in Gabi's voice, but before she could ask further, she was hit from left field.

"Mom? Just before all this happened, Dad said you wanted a divorce."

"Well, talk about changing the subject." Maureen inhaled. "I didn't know he'd told you." She leaned forward, her elbows on the table, her chin in her hands. "There's been so much since then, I almost forgot." She laughed, a nervous sound with no humor.

Gabi sat quietly and waited.

"You don't have to worry about that anymore, Gabi. It was just a … I don't know what to call it. A momentary glitch," she finished weakly.

"Mom, I know you. You didn't make that kind of decision on the spur of the moment."

At the same time, Maureen saw relief flow over Gabi's face, like the sun coming from behind a cloud.

"You know, Mom, you're the center of things."

Maureen started to protest.

Gabi held up her hand. "Everything just feels 'right' when you're here. I don't want to think of the alternative, but you have a right to your own life, too."

Maureen was silent.

"Mom?"

Just at that moment, Bryan came in. "Hey! What's going on? Is this a private confab or just two lazy people?"

Maureen answered him, basking in the warmth of his breezy greeting. "If we were two lazy people, you wouldn't be having dinner, and no, it's not a private confab." Now *this* was normal. Her kids around her, dinner smells wafting from the kitchen, bread baking, her husband on his way home from work. She needed to carry this scene in the center of her mind. She smiled at Gabi and whispered to her, "Don't worry."

Bryan inhaled loudly. "God, it smells so good in here. Not like Burger Heaven."

Gabi sniffed. "So, it's you, that lovely smell of old grease. Please, change and shower before Dad gets home?"

"You'll be sorry when I go back to school. You won't have anyone to pick on." Bryan took the stairs two at a time. Maureen had been so happy to see his sunny nature returning. The first few weeks back in Tampa he had been a different person, quietly sad, insisting on going with Gabi everywhere she went. He had even gone to a couple of her group sessions. But his natural love of people couldn't be destroyed by what had happened to Gabi, and slowly, he had returned to himself except for the times when she saw him sitting quietly, staring off into space.

"You know, when he says school he doesn't mean J.C., Mom."

Maureen sat up straighter. "Meaning?"

Gabi's voice quavered slightly. "Now that the killer is in jail, Bryan wants to go back to U of F in January."

"And you? What about you?" Maureen's voice was small and tight, like she was swallowing the words as she said them.

"We can talk about that later. I can't go back to Gainesville, I know that." She ran her finger down the blade of the knife she had just placed on the table.

"You must be thinking about *something*," Maureen said, her back straight against the chair, the throb in her leg getting stronger.

"I did talk to Aunt Lisa. She said I can stay with her for a while and look at schools out there." At Maureen's look, she laid the knife carefully next to the spoon. "Mom, I asked her. She doesn't know I didn't talk to you first. My counselor suggested maybe a change of scene would be a good idea … not for long, just for a short time, especially now that they won't need a trial in my case …" She trailed off.

Maureen sat very still, taking deep breaths. The news that the rapist had pled guilty and there would be no trial had been the beginning of Gabi's recovery.

"Aunt Lisa said maybe you'd could come out with me, and we could look at schools together. I'm not sure I want to be that far from home, but at least I'd have family close by. We don't have to decide now."

"So you thought of Aunt Lisa? That's better than Alaska or Antarctica," Maureen said, her voice quivering only slightly. "Now that would be a real change of scene."

Gabi sighed, and Maureen sensed the relief in her voice. "Aunt Lisa said she was going to call you about coming out there for Thanksgiving. Then you wouldn't have to do all the work for a change. Maybe she could invite this man who saved your life. Stephen? You sort of left him out of your story."

The garage door went up and Maureen heard Jason's car. "There's your father. Let's get dinner on the table."

"Stay there, Mom. You look tired."

"Gabi?"

"Yes, Mom?"

"How would you like to go out to the beach? Maybe I can answer some of your questions, and we can talk about your plans."

"Sounds good. When?"

"How about tomorrow? I'll call a bed and breakfast, and we can just laze on the beach for a couple of days."

"My two favorite girls," Jason said, standing in the dining room door. "What's for dinner?"

*****

Later, Gabi was alone in the kitchen rinsing the dinner dishes.

"Let me help. I can at least empty the dishwasher," Jason offered, coming in the door.

Gabi looked up from the sink. "What's up, Dad?"

"I thought maybe you'd talk to your mom," Jason said, looking around the kitchen while he held a mixing bowl in his hand.

"Over there," Gabi said, pointing her chin toward the pantry. "Talk to her about what?"

"I like vegetables as much as the next guy, but do you think we could have a roast or something around here pretty soon?"

He looked so pitiful, Gabi burst out laughing. "I'll talk to her, Dad. I didn't notice since I'm a vegetarian anyway, but I guess, now that you mention it, we haven't had any meat around here lately."

"Not since your mom was in California," he said, nearly sneering the word. "The house even smells different—all those new-agey oils and stuff. I caught her putting something on the light bulbs, for Pete's sake. I'd talk to her myself, but she's so sensitive these days, and she listens to you more than me."

"Me?" Gabi asked. "I don't think so."

"Well, you know what I mean. You talk, the two of you."

"Dad, maybe you should give it a try. You and Mom walk around like strangers, so polite, like you're afraid to say anything."

"I guess. Maybe when she's feeling better."

"Why don't you take her out to dinner one night? Then you could have your meat, and she could do what she wants."

"Your mom doesn't like the club."

"Dad, there are restaurants! Good grief. You two need lessons." She hung up the towel. "I'm going up to read a little. Are you OK?"

"Sure, kitten. I'm OK." He gestured at the dishwasher, still fully loaded. "Will you take care of this? I'm sort of out of my element here."

"What did you do while Mom was out West? Use paper plates?"

Jason looked shocked. "I ate at the club. The new chef there is great. Makes a hell of a roast beef." He brushed Gabi's cheek with his lips. "Thanks. I'll go catch the news before I head up."

"Dad?"

Jason stopped in the door.

"Did you meet Stephen?"

Jason's lips pressed into a tight, thin line. "Why don't you ask your mother about him?"

"I did. She doesn't seem to want to talk about it." Gabi picked up the towel and rubbed the stainless sink. "I can understand that. Her accident was really traumatic. Sometimes it's easier to just go forward." Gabi blinked back tears, but Jason didn't notice. His eyes were far away.

"All I know is that when Eleanor and I got there, after Aunt Lisa called, your mom was unconscious, and nobody knew exactly what had happened. Lisa said your mom was out for an early morning walk and the fog moved in. She fell through a gap in the cliff. This guy heard her cry out and jumped in after her." He cleared his throat. "He saved her life, that's all I know."

"Wasn't he hurt, too?"

"His arm was broken in two places, and he had some bruises. The doctor said the water was so cold it kept them from having brain damage."

"But who was he? Did Mom know him?"

"Yes. Gabi, enough questions. Ask your mother," Jason said, abruptly.

"Mom and I are thinking about taking a couple of days and going to the beach. What do you think?"

"When?"

"Well, probably tomorrow."

"I think it's a good idea. I'll be going out of town anyway." He turned and left the kitchen.

Gabi watched him go. There was something strange about all this. Dad didn't seem very happy about the man who had saved his wife from drowning. She put away the dishes and washed down the counters. How many times had she seen her mom doing this while her dad sat in the den and watched sports or news shows? It had seemed fine at the time, but now she wondered why they were together. What was it that had drawn them to each other? Whatever it was, it hadn't lasted. Her hands stopped moving as she thought about that. No, it hadn't lasted. They were like strangers existing in the same house. But as long as they had done what she and Bryan needed, she hadn't noticed. Maybe tomorrow she and her mother would finish their conversation. She wished she had seen her at Emania. What had happened to her out there that she had asked Jason for a divorce? And why had she changed her mind?

Gabi snapped off the lights and stood listening to the night songs of the tree frogs filling the backyard.

Be honest, she thought to herself. You already know the answer to that last question.

*****

Maureen sat in the chaise watching the sand change with every early morning wave that rolled in, the sound of the soft breakers of the Gulf of Mexico only hinting at the booming surf of Oregon. Still, the memories were washing over her with each rivulet, and she wondered how she would possibly explain to Gabi all that had happened to her since the day she opened Dylan's box in the upstairs closet. She squinted down the beach at a couple walking on the packed sand of low tide. The beach at Anna Maria Island was nearly empty, the summer tourists mostly gone, the sun worshipers still in bed. Only a few of the "snow birds" were in residence. Autumn meant aquamarine seas and skies so blue they hurt your eyes. Maureen loved it, this season lifted her heart and sang possibilities. Northerners weren't tuned in to the subtle changing of Florida's seasons. They thought because the leaves didn't turn and frost didn't gild the garden, summer skipped right on through to spring. But it wasn't true. You had to develop an intense awareness of the small changes in air and breeze, shadings of color, the behavior of birds. She drew in the soft air through her mouth.

"Mom, I think I could live out here forever."

"You're a child of my heart, Gabi. I knew the first time I came to the coast that I would never again be without water." She thought back to her first view of the ocean when she came south to go to school. She could never describe that feeling, the freedom she felt in the vastness. "Every time I went back to visit in Illinois, I had this intense claustrophobia. The knowing that I couldn't reach a coast without driving for days was stifling. I always cut my visit short to get back to the water."

"Is it hard for you that Dad doesn't like the beach?"

Maureen wrinkled her nose, a slight tingling letting her know it was time to go in. "It used to be, especially when you kids were little, and I would take you to the beach by myself. But I got used to it. Later, I enjoyed it, those two weeks at the beach in the summer without your dad." She glanced over at Gabi. "Sorry, hon."

"What's to be sorry for? I remember those times too—eating fish sticks from paper plates, tracking sand in the house. Bryan and I built the best sand castles anywhere. Remember those ones we made with the pointy ended paper cups? Fantasy castles, you called them."

Maureen stood and looked down at Gabi. They had slathered her with sun screen, but the new skin on her face was especially vulnerable. With her eyes closed, the asymmetry of her face stood out where the new cheekbone didn't quite match its opposite. But once she opened her eyes and Gabi shone through, no one would notice. "I'm heading in. You're a little pink around the edges. Don't stay out too long."

Gabi smiled, a lazy cat smile, her eyes still closed. "It's only nine in the morning in the middle of winter, Mom."

Maureen stroked the top of Gabi's head. "It's so good to be here with you. I feel lucky." She limped down the beach toward the cottage they were staying in, thinking how the drag of the sand against her foot was good therapy, ignoring the dull throb in her ankle. Only the occasional cry of a gull broke the stillness. The gulls were so much bigger in Oregon, she thought, as she neared the porch. I wonder why that is? She heard the cries increase as someone threw potato chips off a balcony, and the gulls gathered in a huge grey and white cloud, wheeling and complaining in front of the motel. She heard their cries multiplying in her head and remembered their mournful sound as she had plunged through the cliff that foggy day.

Her head ached from the sun and the water's glare as she tripped going up the porch stairs. Inside, she shed her suit and stood for long minutes under the shower, letting the water run into her dry mouth, down her warm body. Afterwards, she fell asleep on the twin bed in the room she shared with

Gabi. Her dreams were full of fog and gulls, and the images of seals surrounded her. She awoke with a start, just as she felt herself falling, her hands grabbing onto the edges of the mattress. Gabi stood in the door toweling her hair.

"Are you OK?"

Maureen nodded. "It was just a dream, nothing important."

"I have them too, and you're wrong. They *are* important. My counselor says they're better addressed than suppressed or something like that." She smiled at her mom. "It's eleven o'clock and I'm starved. Either I fix us some lunch, or I attack the potato chips next door."

They had a quick lunch at the small kitchen table, then roamed through the quirky shops on the island. Gabi talked Maureen into a sun dress on the summer sale rack. Later that night, they ate dinner at a waterfront restaurant where the grouper was so flaky it fell off the fork. They shared a bottle of wine, a first for them and a silent acknowledgment of the closing gap between them.

"Mom, that man over there is looking at you," Gabi whispered, nudging Maureen under the table.

Maureen raised her eyebrows. "I don't think so, Gabi. If he's looking at anyone, it's you. Still, I don't think either of us can see that far very clearly."

"We may have finished off a whole bottle of wine, but I'm not blind. He's looking at you."

"I have to go to the bathroom, Gabi." Maureen got to her feet, swaying slightly. "Thank heavens we walked here. Neither of us would be fit to drive." As she walked past the table Gabi pointed out so subtly, the man smiled.

"You and your sister new around here?" he asked, his voice slurring over the word "around."

Maureen shook her head and went on to the back of the restaurant. He thought Gabi was her sister. What an amazing thing. She giggled, alone in the restroom. Of course it was pretty dark in here. She looked at herself as she dried her hands. Her face was flushed from the sun and the wine, the straps of the white sun dress slipping on her shoulders. Her skin heated even more as she thought of the weight of Stephen's hand on her, his mouth at the base of her throat. She splashed cold water on her face and went back to Gabi.

"No more wine for me," she announced, sitting down.

"He was looking at you, wasn't he?" Gabi asked.

"Both of us, Gabi. I guess he thought he could handle both of us." Her head floated slightly off center, and she took a big gulp of her water.

"I don't know when I'll feel comfortable with a man. My counselor says take my time, but I'm afraid it won't ever happen."

"You're too bright a person to let one sick man keep you from love the rest of your life, Gabi. Your counselor's right. Give yourself time."

"OK, Mom, enough about me. Can we talk about Oregon now?"

*****

Later, Maureen blamed her candor on the wine, but that night she had felt such relief to share her story, from beginning to end, except for her relationship with Stephen. Stephen had to stay in her heart for now. Talking about it wasn't an option. Explaining her experience with Jerome and the haircut had been their undoing. They laughed and cried until even the guy who had been watching them all night gave up and went home. Gabi made her promise to take her to Jerome for a haircut when they went to California.

They walked back to the cottage, and Maureen finished the part about Dylan in the cave while they sat on the porch listening to the quiet swells of the Gulf. Gabi cried quietly as Maureen told about waking up in the hospital to the presence of Jason and Eleanor and the confusion. Then, the anger when she found out what they had kept from her about Gainesville. She recalled the fear and the long plane trip from Oregon after Eleanor called them about Gabi's attack. She told Gabi that she had been remembering the actual accident in Oregon in bits and pieces since she'd been home, but again, she left out her relationship with Stephen.

"What do you think Dylan's message meant, Mom?" Gabi asked, as the tears dried on her cheeks.

"I haven't figured that out yet."

"Dylan showed you that we're all meant to stay our time here, but he didn't tell us why," Gabi lamented. "I feel so confused about why I'm here, what I'm supposed to do." Her voice rose and fell with the water.

"Honey, we've all been through so much this year. Your dad, too. Maybe now we can start to consider the future." She looked hopefully at her daughter. "When you had your … I don't even know how to name it! I knew I needed to be here, and that was enough for now. Let's just enjoy this time together. When we get home, we'll debate our course."

"OK. But I want you to come with me to Oregon. I need to meet these people. Maybe they can help me, too."

"Fair enough. I'll call Brigit and see if there's anything going on this month. It's getting cold out there, and they may have stopped for the winter season."

She heaved herself up out of the chair. "My leg is numb," she mused, rubbing it. "No pain. Maybe wine was the answer all this time." She leaned over and kissed Gabi, knowing they had passed over some kind of line and were now more than mother and daughter. "I'm going to bed. I had a wonderful day."

"Thanks, Mom. I understand some things now that I didn't before. Still, it's really confusing."

Maureen stopped at the door. "I know, but maybe that's what life is in the long run—sorting through the confusion, finding the right path."

"I think you were close to yours, Mom, but now you're drifting off again, coming home and back to the usual with Dad." She put out her hand. "Don't get me wrong. I love Dad. It's just that the two of you seem so …" She stopped. "I don't know. You're so different, and he's still the same."

"I know that, but I'm sure I made the right choice. It's just a different path, not the wrong path." Maureen stepped inside, the door closing firmly behind her.

Chapter Twelve

Maureen and Gabi arrived at Lisa's on a Thursday night. Friday morning they set out to walk the few blocks to Jerome's shop. Maureen stopped frequently, the hills jarring her knitting bones. She regretted leaving her cane.

"Maybe we should have taken a cab," Gabi said, holding her mom by the elbow.

"The doctor said to exercise. I just need to take it slow." The wind dragged at Maureen's hair, strands of red-gold pulling loose and whipping across her eyes. She longed to be cut free of the hair that had grown back into her old style.

Gabi drew her scarf closer around her neck. "It's cold. Will it be like this in Oregon?"

"Probably colder." Maureen looked at the fog hovering below the hills. The Bay was a thick, grey sidewalk. She had a strong urge to walk on it. "We may have to skip the coast road and go another way if this fog keeps up."

Maureen hid a smile at the disappointed look on her daughter's face. She had promised the coast road, telling Gabi how wonderful it was. Now it was up to Lisa. Maureen's inability to drive was a constant source of irritation. She longed for the day when she would be able to go alone somewhere. Anywhere.

She followed Gabi into the shop and was instantly enveloped in the past. She leaned on the door frame for a moment. Her legs were shaking. She held a hand to her chest, soothing her rapidly beating heart.

"Remember, it's Gabrielle," Gabi whispered to Maureen, oblivious of her mother's turmoil.

Maureen pulled herself together. This was about Gabi's new beginning, complete with a more adult name. She burrowed into the warm sound of her daughter's voice. "You know how hard it is for you to remember to call your grandmother Eleanor. This will take time."

She saw Gabi looking over her shoulder, her eyes wide. She turned and was folded like a child into Jerome's arms. Home. Such a feeling, as if she really did have a brother, a twin half. Reluctantly, she pulled back from him and took Gabi by the arm.

"Jerome, I'd like you to meet my daughter, Gabrielle." She faltered slightly.

"You favor your Aunt Lisa," he said, holding Gabi's hand in his. "You're lovely."

Maureen saw him take in all of her daughter, the hurt spaces, the barely visible circles under her eyes. He closed the door and guided them both by their elbows.

"I see you couldn't find anyone to cut your hair back there in Tampa," he teased as he led them to the back of the shop. His soft southern accent flowed over them like slow water. Maureen felt the bones in her legs soften. The constant buzz in her head disappeared. He took her into a curtained booth and leaned back the seat, lifting her legs gently, clucking over the injured one like a mother hen. Maureen thanked him, then closed her eyes, worn out from the trip here, the walk from Lisa's. She heard Jerome and Gabi move off into the same area where he had worked his magic on her when she was a totally different person. His assistant brought Maureen lemon tea and gently massaged her swollen leg, her strong hands warm and healing. The same scents and music filled the air. Maureen settled into the chair, remembering herself, here, less than four months ago. She had been three women since that August day when she called Brigit: the confused and frightened one who came to California looking for answers, the secure beloved of Stephen, and the mother who had put that love aside to help her daughter. Now all three of those were coming together in her, no one path clear through the forest of her life. She fell asleep to the sound of leaves lifting in the breeze.

A wolf-like wail entered Maureen's dream world, and she knew it was her daughter before she could get out of the chair. The fragile cup in her lap crashed to the floor as she fumbled her way through the curtain. People stood rigid in the shop, staring toward the other cubicle. Someone turned off the music. Maureen found Jerome holding her daughter, stroking her hair as he would a small child's, murmuring softly to her. Maureen stood still, her hands out in front of her, not knowing what to do. The cries got softer, dissolving into whimpers.

Jerome gestured to the pile of steamed towels, and Maureen handed him one. He gently wiped Gabrielle's face and leaned her back into the chair. He dimmed the lights and left the room, returning with the ever-ready cup of tea. He handed it to Gabrielle, and she took a sip, looking over the rim at Maureen, her eyes swollen and red below her freshly washed hair.

Maureen stroked her daughter's forehead and dropped a kiss on her wet cheek. "Are you all right?"

Gabrielle nodded and took another sip of tea. She set the cup down and closed her eyes.

Maureen turned to Jerome. He looked stricken. She took his hand in hers. "That's the first time she's cried since she was assaulted," she whispered. She noticed that the music had started up again.

Jerome cleared his throat. "Gabrielle? Shall I do your mother's hair while you rest a little?"

She nodded, her eyes still closed. "I'll be fine," she said, her voice small and sleepy.

"We're right next door. Just call if you need anything." Maureen stroked her daughter's hair, then followed Jerome out of the room.

"What happened?" she asked, sliding back into the chair.

Jerome leaned her head back into the shampoo bowl, his hazel eyes shadowed. "She was so tight in her neck muscles and shoulders. I gave her a massage, like I gave you. When I leaned her forward and put my hands on her neck, she came up out of the chair screaming. The pain in her eyes . . ." he trailed off. "I hope I never see that again."

Maureen put her hand over his soapy one. "She's been in therapy and group sessions since it happened and never been able to cry. She hasn't let anyone male touch her either, except for Bryan. I saw you holding her when I came in the room. It was one of the happiest moments of my life." Maureen closed her eyes and let Jerome's hands ease the pain from her neck and shoulders.

Stephen's face loomed in her mind as Jerome worked.

*****

She thought back to her phone conversation with Brigit. At the end, she had asked about Stephen, and Brigit told her he was in Europe working with another sculptor.

"He'll probably stay there a year or two," Brigit had continued, her voice like cold water. Maureen's hand had loosened on the receiver and loss descended on her as she pictured Stephen in a stone cottage in France, the one they had talked about sharing together. She envisioned sun sprinkling through leaves, a small grape arbor on the side of the hill, and the perfect light flowing in the windows like amber honey. Brigit's voice continued in the distance, and Maureen had strained to hear her, knowing she had no right to these feelings. She had forfeited them when she returned to her family.

"Maureen? Are you still there?" Brigit had asked.

"Yes, I'm sorry. I drifted off for a minute. I do that sometimes these days. Please, repeat what you said about the group that's meeting around Thanksgiving."

Brigit told her about the two young women who were coming for the spirituality and meditation classes the week before Thanksgiving.

"It won't be specifically about your daughter's problem," she had warned.

"That's fine. She has her group and her therapist for that," Maureen replied. "Gabi wants to look at schools, and Lisa and I are going with her. The timing is perfect."

"Wonderful." Maureen had sensed a thaw in her voice as they spoke about Gabi. "Why don't you come here with her and then stay for Thanksgiving? We'd love to have you."

Maureen had hesitated. "I don't know, Brigit. So many things happened to me there, wonderful and terrible things. Please, send me the information, and I'll let you know."

*****

That had been three weeks ago, and now, here they were starting off the same way she had months earlier. Maureen sat quietly, her hair drying while Jerome finished with Gabi. She jerked from her reverie at Gabi's voice.

"Mom! It doesn't even look like you."

"What do you mean?" She leaned forward toward the mirror. "Oh, I see," she said, putting her hands up to her face. "I forgot you hadn't seen me in my new incarnation. What do you think?"

"You're beautiful. And you look like Jerome's twin sister, maybe just a little older. I can see why you fell in love with him."

Maureen blushed.

"Really?" Jerome asked. "She forgot to tell me."

Maureen studied her daughter. "And look at you. You look wonderful. You're definitely a Gabrielle now."

Gabrielle swung her chin length hair back and forth. It swished like a velvet curtain, the red sheen on her dark hair sparking fire under the lights and mirrors. She looked like Lisa and Jason mixed together, set off by Maureen's translucent skin. The side part let her hair skim down over the left side of her face, laying shadow where the thin scars traced her cheekbone. She did look like a Gabrielle. Maureen resolved to call her that even in her thoughts, until it became second nature.

"You two stay out of trouble," Jerome said, admiring them. "You're a high octane pair."

Gabrielle kissed him on the cheek. "Thanks," she whispered.

Maureen noted they were all three the same height, like three sides of a statue.

"Anytime. Let me know if you stay here for school."

Gabrielle shivered. "If this weather is any indication, I may have to go back to Florida after all."

Maureen hugged the words to her, realizing only in that moment how she had been dreading the loss of this child to California. They headed out into the damp afternoon, waving behind them to Jerome who stood slumped in the door, watching them go. They had lunch on the way home and stopped in a small grocery to get some things for dinner. Maureen bustled in the kitchen for an hour, then settled in one of Lisa's deep chairs to read. Gabrielle was asleep on the couch.

Around four o'clock Maureen woke, her head back on the cushioned chair. She rubbed her sore neck, then saw Gabrielle standing by the window. It was already feeling like dusk. "I remember the first time I was here," she said quietly. "The beauty struck me dumb. Then I had my appointment with Jerome. I was primed for something big."

Gabrielle turned from the window, the waning light caught in the sheen of her hair. "Tell me about the ceremony again. I don't know what to expect."

"I don't think it will be the same for you," Maureen said. "Did you look at Brigit's letter?"

"Yes. I'm nervous, though. Dad said this went against what the Church teaches."

"He said that?"

"Mom, sometimes you're just in your own little world."

Maureen heard the exasperation in her daughter's voice.

"It's not just him," Gabrielle went on. "Grandmother said the same thing."

Maureen caught the slip back into "Grandmother" that signaled Gabrielle's real confusion. Her dad and her grandmother, two powerful family icons invoking the full power of the Church. She chose her words carefully.

"Gabrielle, I'm not trying to change your faith or turn you into a New Age groupie." She paused, running her hands through her hair. "Words are so inadequate to convey what I feel. The work I did with the women in Oregon? It made God bigger for me." She hesitated, tried again. "For me, now, it's a universe, not just a small insulated world. My spiritual life includes so much more. It doesn't exclude." She waved her hands in front of her, erasing words. "I give up. I just can't explain it. You're an adult woman, Gabrielle. You'll decide for yourself."

Gabrielle knelt by her mother's chair. "OK, Mom. I'll try to go with an open mind. Right now, I'm confused. This hair, when it touches my face? I feel like I've turned into a different person."

Maureen touched her daughter's sleek head. For a brief moment, hardly a whisper, the bodies of seals swam through her mind. "You're just seeing more of yourself. I feel it, too. When I went home? I kind of forgot about the rest of me, as if I left it behind in California."

"Left what, Sis?" Lisa asked, coming down the hallway.

They both jumped. "We didn't hear you come in," Gabrielle said, getting up to hug her aunt.

"Well, I am in and I'm starving." She looked at them. "My God, you're both beautiful."

"Thanks, Aunt Lisa. Jerome says I look like you."

Lisa blushed. "Let's go out to eat."

"If you don't mind, Lisa, Gabi and I … sorry. Gabrielle and I had a really long day. I made some chicken salad, and we found some beautiful tomatoes in your fridge."

Lisa looked relieved. "That sounds perfect. I'll go down the street and get some fresh bread."

"I can do that, Aunt Lisa." Gabrielle got her coat.

"Once I get the weather report, we'll decide on our route for tomorrow and we're off." Lisa hugged Maureen. "Thanksgiving with my two favorite people. I'm really excited. It's usually a pretty lonely holiday for me if I don't get to Florida." She looked at Gabrielle framed in the door. "I feel sorry for the rest of the family."

"Don't, Aunt Lisa. I think Dad and Eleanor are looking forward to eating at the club in peace and quiet," Gabrielle's face fell. "And Bryan's having Thanksgiving dinner with his new girlfriend's family. All the old traditions are dying." Her voice shook.

"But we'll put new ones in their place, and you'll help make them. It will be exciting," Maureen reassured her.

The door closed softly behind Gabrielle, her sigh lingering in the room. "I'm not sure she buys that, Maureen."

*****

After dinner, they watched the report of unusually clear November weather. The weatherman said it would last about three days.

"See, Mom? It was meant."

Lisa agreed to drive the coast highway so they could stop and see the redwoods.

The weather stayed beautiful for the trip north, and Gabrielle hadn't been disappointed in anything. The redwoods took her breath away, as they had her mother's. They saw moose foraging for the winter, their thick brown coats standing out against the yellow grass. They stopped at a different motel, a place without a whirlpool boiling at the bottom of a cliff. That night they built a fire and stayed up late, snuggled together on the king sized bed. Maureen and Lisa told stories of their growing up years, stories Gabrielle had never heard. When Lisa told her about Maureen's trip onto the altar, Gabrielle was stunned. Even now, girls were just being allowed to read during the Mass.

She looked at her mother and shook her head. "I just can't see it. I know you're strong, but you never seemed like the . . . I don't know, . . . the adventurous type. I can't even imagine you as a kid."

Lisa reached for her purse. "Look at this." She pulled a picture out of the back of her wallet.

Maureen took it from her. It was old and frayed, the sepia image fading into the background, but Maureen recognized it. It was the two of them in a dime store picture booth, an old torn curtain hanging behind them, their hair in pony tails. Lisa was sixteen, she, two years younger. "Oh my gosh. Where did you get this?"

"I've been carrying it since we were kids. Look at those grins. We had just finished root beer floats at the counter, and we were wearing *Evening In Paris* perfume."

Maureen could smell the sample perfume on their wrists that had choked them in the small booth.

Maureen touched Lisa's hand. "It was the end of summer, right before you met Roger." Maureen caught a quick breath.

"It's OK. I keep this because it was such an innocent time. Look at those faces. Not a clue as to what would come."

"Who's Roger? What was to come?" Gabrielle was in the dark, watching her mother and aunt.

Their eyes glistened with tears.

"Roger was Aunt Lisa's one and only true love," Maureen began, flashing a questioning look at her sister. Lisa nodded. "He died on the way to Vietnam."

"Oh, Aunt Lisa. I didn't know. You never talked about him."

"I couldn't. Not for a long time, except to your mom. She knew everything. Besides, there wasn't much to it."

"Not much to it? Only three years of your lives and all that love." Maureen hugged Lisa.

"Our parents didn't approve. He wanted to get married, but I was too young. So, he joined the Marines. A year later, while I waited for him, going to school at Berkeley, he was killed in a training accident. Your mom went to college in Florida that same year and met your dad. The rest is history."

"You never found anyone else?" Gabrielle couldn't keep the wonder out of her voice.

"Well, I thought I had when I married Larry." She scrunched her face in distaste. "That made me question my judgement."

"I don't remember him. I was so little."

Lisa shrugged. "You didn't miss anything. Since the divorce, I've dated lots of guys, but it never felt right. Maybe because Roger was in a shrine, and shrines are hard to compete with."

"It could still happen, Aunt Lisa. You're really great looking for your age and stuff."

Lisa and Maureen raised their eyebrows at the same time, a typical Quinn expression.

Gabrielle giggled. "I have that same look. It drives my friends nuts. You know what I mean. You and mom are both foxy chicks. But Mom has Dad." She looked at Maureen. "At least for now, she doesn't need anyone else. Maybe we can find somebody for you."

"Thanks, Gabrielle. I do just fine by myself."

"Jerome has a tone in his voice when he talks about you, doesn't he, Mom?"

"Jerome?" Maureen thought. "As a matter of fact …"

"Quit, you guys. He *is* interested, but he's six years younger than me."

"So? Mom, tell her. Age is insignificant."

"Age is insignificant, Sis," Maureen responded, robot-voiced.

Lisa rolled over to her side of the bed and switched off the light. "Early start, guys. Let's cut the chatter. Tomorrow's a busy day."

"Maybe Brigit can get a coven together to put a spell on you and Jerome."

"Gabrielle! What a thing to say!"

"I'm sorry, Mom. That's what Grandmother said for me to look out for. A coven. She's just worried about you and all this new stuff you're into."

"Since when has Eleanor been someone you pay close attention to anyway?"

"Well, Dad seemed to agree with her." Gabrielle slid off the side of the bed. "And you've got to admit you haven't been the same."

"For God's sake, Gabi. Who would be with all we've been through this year? What does Bryan say about all this?"

Gabrielle crawled into the fold-out bed. "*Gabrielle,* Mom. Bryan is Bryan. He says do what feels right and that's all that matters. It makes Dad crazy. Anyway, I was just observing. Dad and Eleanor are just worried because they love you."

Maureen hoped she was the only one who heard Lisa's muffled "hurumph" from under the blanket.

Chapter Thirteen

They spent three crystalline days meandering up the coast. On the third day, it turned chill and wet, the weather deteriorating rapidly as they arrived at Emania on Tuesday afternoon. At dinner, the fireplace drove away the damp as Brigit said a simple grace over the hearty soup and crusty home-baked bread. Lisa produced a red wine they'd bought on the way, and they lingered at the table into the evening, sharing stories with Gabrielle.

"I still don't understand what happened to Mom here. She came back home so changed. I blamed it on the accident, when I thought about it."

"Blamed what, Gabrielle?" Lisa asked.

"We'll have plenty of time for that," Brigit interjected, as she came back from taking a phone call. "We've had a bad weather report—fog all the way up— so the other women have canceled. It looks like it will just be us and, of course, Mary Virginia. If its OK with you, Gabrielle, we'll go ahead with tonight's planned session on massage."

Gabrielle nodded, a little hesitantly Maureen thought.

"Your mother offered to drop out of the group if it would make you more comfortable."

Gabrielle shook her head. She had retreated inside herself again.

"When do we start, Brigit?" Lisa asked.

"In an hour? It's as good a time as any, I think." Brigit looked at the three of them. "Any objections?"

Lisa shifted in her chair. "Maybe you should give us a little synopsis of what you plan to do."

Brigit looked at Gabrielle. "May I talk freely?"

Again, Gabrielle nodded.

"Well, it seems to me that we need to help Gabrielle deal with the trauma of her attack." Brigit shifted in her chair and looked directly into Gabrielle's eyes. "From what you said about your experience in the beauty shop, things are lying just under the surface."

Gabrielle shrugged, her hands clenching into fists in her lap.

"Let's go into the other room." Brigit stood as the increasing strength of the rain sent swirls of smoke down the chimney.

Maureen followed. The dampness invaded her limbs making her walk like an old woman. She sat heavily in the chair near the fireplace. The memory of Stephen kneeling in front of her caught at her throat as Gabrielle settled near her feet. Maureen stroked her daughter's hair, watching the fire pick out the red strands, turning them to bronze ribbons. Wind rattled at the windows, sought entrance under the roof and went away howling.

Brigit's soft voice lifted through the pine scented room. She thanked the gods and goddesses for their dinner, the warmth of the fire, the friendship and love each gave to the other. Then she threw fresh herbs on the fire, their pungent scent filling the air. She lifted a book from the table and began to read, the sound of her voice carrying to them on the smells of pine and rosemary:

This is the time of the harvest, leave-taking and sorrow. The season of barrenness is upon us, yet we give thanks for that which we have reaped and gathered. The end of a cycle has come. We enter our resting season.

Brigit closed her eyes. "May all of us here enter into our quiet time, our time of reflection on the ways of this world and how we are to live in it. May we show wisdom and compassion with our sister who has suffered at the hands of one of your beings. May she go inside herself to find the strength to trust again."

Maureen's love threatened to consume her as she watched Gabrielle squeeze her eyes closed in concentration. She knew how hard it was to take in the prayer Brigit was saying. It was so different from the rote words of Sunday Mass, this talking directly with God about specific problems. The wind whirled around the house enclosing them in a cocoon of warmth and light, the shallow breathing of all five women blending in the room. Lisa was nearly asleep in her chair. Mary Virginia took a quilt from her lap and laid it on the rag rug. She covered it with a sheet, handing Gabrielle a big, fluffy towel. Gabrielle took the towel and went into the next room.

Brigit set several jars of oil near the fire where they absorbed the flames, glowing like liquid gems. "Maureen, do you think you can remember what you learned?"

Maureen picked up the jar of green oil. "I remember this one is for the heart area. And the gold? I think the abdomen?"

Brigit nodded. "Remember how stiff you were with having your body touched?"

Maureen blushed. "I remember."

"Gabrielle's trauma has her feeling that a thousand times over. We're going to help her over that, one stroke at a time." She stopped talking as Gabrielle came back in the room, the towel wrapped tight around her and tucked in snug above her breasts.

"Please lay on your stomach, Gabrielle. And promise that you'll let us know any time you feel uncomfortable."

Gabrielle burrowed her face into the fire-warmed quilt.

"Maureen, you'll be at her head, Lisa at her feet." Brigit handed each of them a jar of the now warm oil, then knelt at Gabrielle's side. Flute music drifted from the stereo across the room, the notes creating a small clearing in a forest. Mary Virginia closed the door behind her as she left.

"Your mom will massage your neck and shoulders, Gabrielle. Your aunt will do your feet and legs. I'm going to talk to you while they work. Stop us anytime you feel the need." She nodded at Maureen and Lisa. Maureen tried to remember the intricate movements she had learned to ease knotted muscles and soothe stress. She began with her daughter's shoulders, prayed she wouldn't trigger the same emotions Jerome had in touching her neck. As she stroked the fragile bones in Gabrielle's upper back, she heard Brigit's soothing voice blending with the flute, describing the stress and fear flowing out into the universe, the love and care flowing into Gabrielle's body. She felt her fingers moving with the music and Brigit's voice. In the orange glow from the fire, Lisa's hands stroked golden oil down Gabrielle's legs: long sure strokes that passed over the heels and down the soles of her feet.

Brigit began to talk of the goodness in the world, the goodness in Gabrielle's soul that would spread out and around her as soon as the fear was gone. Maureen felt her daughter's shoulders relax, then shudder as the soft cries of a wounded child flowed from her into the quilt. She moved her hands up to the back of Gabrielle's head, her thumbs pressing into her neck, just below the fragile skull. Later, as she soothed the scars on Gabrielle's face, cries rose from her daughter like gull's wings. The sound flowed out into the room and was absorbed into the fire and the music. They continued their work for an hour, until every bit of anger, fear and despair were gone from the relaxed and glowing young body. Maureen's back ached with tiredness, and then she heard the most wonderful sound in the world, the soft, childlike snores of Gabrielle, asleep on the quilt. The women wrapped her carefully, slid a pillow under her head, laid a blanket over her and left her in front of the fire. Maureen hobbled to the stairs, too tired to say good night. Brigit's smile said it all. Two days and then it would be Thanksgiving. She had a lot to be thankful for. Maureen fell asleep with the scent of evergreen on her hands, the sounds of her daughter being reborn in her ears.

The next day, the storm worsened. Thunderous surf slammed into the cliffs as the winds and rain battered the house. Inside it was warm and scented with apples from pies baking for "the feast," as they had begun calling Thanksgiving. Throughout the day, Brigit led exercises in meditation, visualization, and the slow, voluptuous movements of Tai Chi. Maureen did her best with the physical part, but as she settled into the routine of meditation, peace descended on her spirit. She had felt at home the moment Brigit introduced her to these concepts months ago. The last day with Stephen, before she was told of Gabrielle's assault, they had meditated together. They had prayed for their future, for Maureen to have the strength to heal and face Jason with her decision. Maureen chased the thoughts out of her space, telling herself she would deal with them later. As they finished the session, Maureen saw Lisa looking at her, looking into her. It was a relief. Lisa knew what she was thinking, and it was OK. She looked next to her at Gabrielle and laughed aloud. Her daughter was sitting straight up, her legs crossed just so, her hands held just so, and she was sound asleep. Lisa leaned over to her niece and put her arms around her, waking her gently.

Dinner was quiet that night, everyone awash in their own thoughts. Mary Virginia served soup and salad, followed by a custard, its cinnamon sauce scenting the air. Vivaldi played on the stereo.

"Why is it some foods smell like home, even if your mother never made them?" Lisa asked no one in particular.

"It's the home we wish for or imagine," Brigit said. "Like Thanksgiving. We have this picture of chestnuts roasting, Dad carving the turkey, everyone warm and cozy. Reality, for most people, is far different."

"I think that we keep trying is a courageous thing," Maureen said. Something in her voice caught their attention.

"Mom always tried," Gabrielle said quietly. "But she never thought she succeeded."

"I didn't?" Maureen asked, surprised.

"Mom, c'mon. Last year the turkey was dried out because Dad's golf was going so well he played three more holes. The year before …"

Maureen held up her hand. "Stop! I can't take it. You're not going all the way back, are you?"

Lisa laughed. "She's right, Maureen. I think you saw this picture of the happy family once in Better Homes and Gardens, and you keep waiting for it to show up at your dinner table. Every year, one of us spoils the picture."

Sadness tinged the edges of Maureen's joy at being teased by Gabrielle. Was it so obvious, the striving for the "happy family" picture? Every year she had hosted anyone who wanted to come, reveling in days of cooking, crisp linens, games in the den afterwards, football down at the park. It was true that Jason was either late or hunkered down in front of the television, but it hadn't always been that way. It seemed like there were always extras at the dinner table, especially as the kids got older. Friends, stranded classmates with no solid place to call home.

Jason sort of got lost in the crowd.

"Mom?"

Maureen felt Gabrielle's hand on her shoulder. "It's OK. You did a wonderful job. We depend on you for that. No one else even tried. We're just teasing. I don't know what we'd do if you didn't make the effort. That's why this year feels so strange."

"Strange but OK?" Brigit questioned.

"OK for this year," Gabrielle responded. "But I like tradition. It will be nice to be back to normal."

"And what's normal for you?" Brigit asked, her voice mildly curious but not threatening.

"Mom and Dad at each end of the table. There for us when we come home. I imagine it stretching down the road like an endless movie, the table expanding to hold my children and Bryan's children." Gabrielle stretched her arms wide, encompassing her image of their future.

"Maureen, is that your picture, too?" Brigit probed, her voice a little sharper.

Maureen looked at Brigit, a warning in her eyes. "This year has not been easy for our family, Brigit. I think we all look forward to getting back to normal."

"I'm really glad you feel that way, Mom. We were all worried that we were losing you. And how about you Aunt Lisa? Will you be coming to Tampa more often now that you're going to slow down and all that?"

"Who said I was slowing down? Just changing focus, that's all." She looked across at Maureen. "And I'll see you both more often no matter where you are."

"I'll be in Tampa, too, Aunt Lisa," Gabrielle said, missing Lisa's point. "This weather is wonderful for a couple of days. Book reading, meditation, all of that. But I need to get back to the sunshine. So, Thanksgiving in Tampa next year. You could come too, Brigit. It would be a real change for you."

Brigit smiled, a smile that didn't reach her eyes. "I promise. Wherever Maureen is next year, there I'll be for Thanksgiving. Let's all promise the same."

"That's easy." Gabrielle raised her glass. "To Thanksgiving in Tampa."

Maureen sipped her wine, the tears pooling in the corners of her eyes splintering the candle's flame. She felt Brigit's eyes on her. Maureen didn't feel about Oregon like Gabrielle did. Right now she felt home, howling wind, battering rain and all. She felt Gabi retreating back into her comfort zone, despite her brave words to Maureen at the beach. No one was going to give her permission to live her life but herself.

Thanksgiving morning, Brigit worked with Gabrielle, teaching her some of the skills Maureen and Lisa had already learned. Maureen peeled sweet potatoes while Lisa made the scalloped oysters, a Quinn family Thanksgiving tradition. Mary Virginia was toasting bread for the stuffing. Maureen leaned back in her chair and closed her eyes, inhaling the scented air, feeling the warmth of the potatoes under her hands.

"Look at her, Lisa." Mary Virginia was eyeing Maureen with the satisfied look of a true friend. "She really gets content with this cooking thing."

"We always said Maureen should have her own restaurant. Well, everyone except Mom, that is." She looked affectionately at her sister, who still sat with her eyes closed, bliss radiating from her.

"Why not your mom?" Mary Virginia asked.

"We were supposed to be taken care of, not working class," Lisa answered her. "I guess that's why she doesn't talk much about her daughter, the lawyer."

Maureen opened her eyes. "What would Mom have to say about herself if she acknowledged how well you take care of yourself? She's being protective of her image."

"I know you're right, but I still long for the day." Lisa laughed a short, unhappy laugh. "I need to keep practicing that self-congratulation thing Brigit taught us. I have the damndest time getting that right."

Mary Virginia licked bread crumbs from her fingers. "Don't feel bad. For whatever reason, it's the toughest part for all of us." She looked toward the door. "Even Brigit," she whispered.

Lisa raised her eyebrows. "I can't imagine. She seems so sure of herself."

"You said that about me, too," Maureen put in, "until we came here and started telling each other the truth."

Lisa poked a fork at the oysters she was laying on their bed of crackers and butter. "And Mom? Do you think she'll ever tell the truth?"

Maureen thought a minute. "Probably not. But we have to just take her how she is for now. Who knows? Maybe next year, she'll be out here." She peeled the deep orange flesh of the next potato and laid it carefully in the buttered casserole. "I do know, I'm afraid I'll be too late to make peace with her if I don't do it soon, and I don't think I could handle that."

"Is something wrong with your mother?"

"No, nothing like that. At least not that we know of. Mom kind of does her own thing. But she is getting older." She trailed off. "Maybe Christmas. That's a good time for mending fences, right Lisa?"

"If I didn't have so few of these oysters, I'd throw one at you, Maureen. Don't remind me of Christmas. It's the hardest time of year for me. I just want to enjoy Thanksgiving. OK?"

Maureen heard the tears in Lisa's voice. "I'm sorry." She picked up a napkin and dabbed at Lisa's face, both of them laughing as the sweet potatoes on the napkin decorated Lisa's cheeks. "Maybe you could come to Tampa for Christmas. Actually, I think you should think about moving there."

"Are you nuts? Live in that heat? I don't think so." Her glance traveled to the clouded windows where the heat from the kitchen obscured the rain. "Still, sunshine might be nice in the winter. Maybe I could commute."

"Commute where?" Gabrielle asked, coming into the steamy room.

"Aunt Lisa was just being silly," Maureen answered, the happiness she felt as she looked at Gabrielle's glowing face an early Christmas gift. "How's the meditation coming?"

"I like it. I didn't think I would, but the music helps a lot." She grabbed a piece of potato out of the bowl. "I'm starved. Is all this food for tonight?"

Mary Virginia lifted the lid on a big soup pot simmering on the back of the stove. "Clam chowder in about half an hour," she announced, tasting.

"Lisa, save us some of those crackers."

Gabrielle rubbed a clear spot on the window glass. "It's stopped raining." She turned to Maureen. "Mom? Can you show me where you had your accident?"

Maureen's contentment slid from her. She had been secretly glad the weather had kept them indoors. She was afraid to go near the edge, see that surf swirling under her feet.

Mary Virginia saw her hesitation. "There's a wall around it, Maureen. It'll be OK if its what you want."

Maureen sighed. "How about after lunch, if it clears a little?"

"Great. I'll take a shower now." Gabrielle inhaled. "Oh. It smells so good in here. Just like home." She let the kitchen door swing closed behind her.

Maureen looked around her. Just like home? With three of them working together, preparations for Thanksgiving were fun, punctuated with conversation, help, laughter. She pictured herself in Tampa, alone in the kitchen, everyone showing up an hour before dinner, eating in thirty minutes what it had taken her three days to prepare. She smiled at Lisa and Mary Virginia. Oh, this was definitely not like home.

"I'm swooning," Brigit cried in mock movie star fashion, swaying into the kitchen. "The smells. I've died and gone to heaven." She closed her eyes and inhaled. "I wish I could get this smell in a spray."

"Your next project," Mary Virginia answered, affection coating her voice. "Lunch will be ready in twenty-five minutes."

"You're an angel," Brigit responded, putting her arm around Mary Virginia's shoulders. "I don't know what I'd do without you."

"Lose lists?" Mary Virginia guessed, laughing.

Maureen closed her eyes again, leaning far back in her chair. When did she and Jason ever banter? Their conversations concerned paying the bills, whether or not she would go to whatever party was coming up. Even the kids had been off limits in their rare discussions. He just wanted her to handle it. She looked up. Brigit and Mary Virginia were both looking at her. She called up a wan smile.

"That's pitiful," Brigit said. "Isn't that the most pitiful smile you ever saw? Lisa? Mary Virginia? What can we do to improve that smile?"

Maureen was laughing now, basking in the love and warmth in the room. She would think about Tampa later. She threw back her head, raised her hand theatrically to her forehead. "I'll think about it tomorrow," she intoned in her best southern accent. She stopped, the threat of the oyster in Lisa's hand putting an end to her Scarlet O'Hara.

*****

Lunch over, Maureen went to the window, disappointed that the rain had stopped. Fog shrouded everything beyond three feet, but Gabrielle appeared next to her wearing a slicker, holding one out to her mother. Her eyes were shadowed under the rain gear.

"Mom? If you don't want to, I'll understand, but I need to see where all this happened."

Maureen hugged Gabrielle, the slicker crackling under her hands. "It's OK." She thought of herself going to the apartment in Gainesville, trying to understand what had happened there to Gabrielle so she could help her. She opened the door, breathing deep of the clotted air, then waited for her daughter to pass. She pulled the slicker tight around her, hands shaking as they rounded the corner of Stephen's studio. Fog obscured the garden, leafless grape vines wound tightly around each other.

"What's that, Mom?"

"Part of the studio," Maureen answered shortly, looking toward the bluff. The surf roared like a train in a tunnel. Fog covered everything, a grey shawl revealing a shape here and there, then quickly covering it again. She took a step back. "I don't know about this. It's too much like ..." Maureen stopped, rubbing her hands across her eyes. "I couldn't see then and I can't see now."

Then, the fog parted and straight ahead, up the rise, was a low wall of white granite. "That must be it. It's not as far as I remember. I must have walked in circles that day." Gabrielle held onto her hand as they walked the open path. A stray beam of sun glittered on the wall. The wall was waist high, smooth and undulating like a sculptured wave. Maureen hung back as Gabrielle approached and peered over, her indrawn breath audible to Maureen several feet behind her. She turned to her mother, the scars on her face visible against the pallor of her skin.

"You couldn't have survived this. It must be another place."

Maureen pulled even with Gabrielle and leaned forward, her breath caught tight in her chest. She laid her hand on the edge of the wall, felt lines in the smooth edge as she forced herself to look down. Her throat closed at the sight of the swiftly whirling water filled with debris of all kinds; driftwood fragments, seaweed, pieces of glass and netting. She sat abruptly on the damp ground, facing the ocean.

"Mom? Are you OK? I'm so sorry. This was a terrible idea."

Maureen shook her head. "I'll be fine. Just a little weak in the knees. I don't have a memory of my rescue, just the actual falling and what I saw."

"What did you see?"

Maureen hesitated, then decided. "I told you before that I saw Dylan, Gabrielle. Clear as a bell." She turned her thoughts inward. "He was so beautiful. Like an angel, only real. Fully himself."

"Stay there, Mom. I'm going in to get some help."

"I'm fine, Gabrielle. It's all true. I did see him and he spoke to me."

At Gabrielle's look she amended herself. "Not aloud, of course. But I knew what he was telling me."

"You said he told you to live. To go back and live the life you were meant to. But Dad said you had a really bad blow to the head, and you were hallucinating. Is this what he meant? Did you tell him about Dylan?"

"I tried to." Her eyes closed, remembering Jason's sickroom voice as he asked the doctor to give her a sedative. "Anyway. That's his explanation for it. Not mine." She saw Gabrielle's blue lips quivering. "Go in, I'm fine. I'm coming." She put her hand against the granite and lifted herself. In the watery reflection of the sun, she saw one word carved into the side of the stone, facing the beach. She leaned closer. *Beloved*. She felt her heart thud against her ribs, her lungs stretch with the effort to breathe. Beloved. Stephen. He built this wall. It was not ordinary. It was more like a headstone. No. Not that. A monument. Her heart stopped, then resumed a steady beat. It was a memorial to their love, this place. She heard Gabrielle's voice from a distance, then felt herself being lifted under the arms by gentle hands, voices that fell like birds around her. They brought her inside, tucked her into the chair in front of the fire and piled her with blankets. Someone held a cup of hot mint tea to her mouth and she sipped, feeling the burning on her tongue.

"Mom, I'm sorry. I didn't realize. I'm so sorry."

She roused herself at the misery in her daughter's voice.

"Don't be. I needed to remember. It's important. I told you that, but I forgot it for myself."

Brigit's voice cleared the fog away. "Your mom just needs a little rest, Gabrielle. Why don't you help me in the kitchen for a bit while she naps."

Maureen closed her eyes. She watched as a movie unreeled before her. The warm room dissolved. She was in the water, watching Dylan retreat to the back of the cave. Violently, she was sucked up into a battering whirlpool. Her bones seemed to separate from her muscles, a wrenching pain not unlike childbirth. Bits and pieces of trash flung themselves at her, stinging her eyes and nose. Her lungs flattened, gave up the last of their air, and she knew the true meaning of blackness. But something was there, a force dragging her upward, through the snarling, clogged waters. Her lungs opened, sucking the searing freezing air and water into themselves. Shapes, black and sleek, were all around her, pushing her up, bumping against her. Then she saw legs, felt arms around her and heard voices, Stephen's voice, Dylan's voice, telling her to fight, to swim. She kicked with all of her remaining strength. Excruciating pain stabbed into her legs and feet, like shards of ice. And then, blackness. Blessed dark. She cried out, opened her eyes to the warm glow of the room, smelled the scent of roasting turkey. When she closed her eyes again, she slept. This time in peace.

Chapter Fourteen

Fog drifted in closer, staying now, pushing the dark against the walls. Inside, the house was luminous with candles. Rich smells from the kitchen permeated every corner, and the tang of cedar from the fireplace wafted over the trestle table laid with creamy linen. Nestled in pine boughs, honeycomb candles glowed on the red jewels of fresh cranberries. The five women joined hands, Lisa and Gabrielle stretching their arms over the sixth place setting that remained empty across from Maureen. Brigit explained that she wasn't expecting anyone, but it was a tradition to keep a place for a wandering traveler. Seeing the banks of fog bumping the windows as Brigit gave thanks, Maureen was sure the place would remain empty.

Brigit squeezed Maureen's hand. "Would you like to go next?"

Maureen bowed her head. So much turmoil, but so much to be thankful for. She opened her eyes and looked around the table. "I give full and heartfelt thanks for the gift of each of you in my life and for the gift of life itself."

Each woman gave thanks, Gabrielle saying the Catholic form of grace as Lisa held her hand from one side, Brigit the other. The serenity of Mozart drifted from the speakers as Mary Virginia carved the turkey, and from that point on, the only sounds were groans of appreciation. For the first time, Maureen didn't think about who was missing, even with the empty chair right across from her. It was perfect just like it was.

Nearly an hour passed as they ate and talked. Slowly, forks dropped on plates, chairs scooted back, little sounds of contentment escaped into the room.

"Mary Virginia has a surprise dessert," Brigit announced, striking her fork on a wine glass. The ping of crystal was drowned in groans of denial.

"No more, please," Gabrielle begged.

Mary Virginia laughed. "We can eat it later. I just have to bring it in now."

Maureen helped Brigit clear the table. Mary Virginia entered the candle lit room, the blue of brandy fire a halo around her face. She looked like an ancient queen at a ritual as she set the plum pudding carefully in the middle of the table.

"Traditionally, I make this for Christmas, but now seemed the right time." The flames dwindled to a small tongue, then died.

"Can I have just a small piece?" Gabrielle asked.

"Me too, please. Just a little." Voices chimed in from around the table.

Mary Virginia whisked small crystal bowls off the side table. She carved soft spoons of pudding into the bowls, put dollops of clotted cream on the top and passed one to each. Only the sound of spoons scraping crystal broke the quiet.

"Every cook's dream," Mary Virginia said. "Total respectful silence."

"I never trusted anyone who didn't like to eat," Lisa said. "Tonight, this is total trust. It's absolutely orgasmic." She looked next to her.

"My thought exactly," Gabrielle sighed.

Maureen drew in her breath, then subsided. "Me, too," she said in a small voice. "Me, too."

The table broke up into laughter. They herded Mary Virginia into an easy chair. "The cook doesn't clean," Gabrielle commanded.

At her mother's look, she shrugged. "There's always room for new rules."

"And getting rid of old ones?" her mother asked.

"Maybe so," Gabrielle answered. "I'm just not sure which ones." She kissed Maureen on the cheek. "I have to run upstairs for a few minutes. You wash, I'll dry."

Maureen smiled to herself as Gabrielle took the stairs two at a time. Sometimes she envied her daughter's youth. She ran hot water in the sink, watching the steam fog the window from the inside. No, that wasn't true. She didn't envy her youth, just her energy. And knowing what she knew now. If she had that knowledge earlier, what would she have done with it? She laughed at herself as she dunked the glasses in the hot, soapy water. Probably nothing. Everybody learns alone and acts alone in the final analysis, though being here made her think that it was possible to share the burden.

Lisa whipped into the kitchen, flicking Maureen with the towel. "Just like old times."

Maureen laughed. They finished the dishes in quiet companionship, the stereo still playing Mozart, the candles slowly burning down.

Lisa was drying the last pot when Gabrielle came downstairs, slowly, one foot in front of the other. Maureen thought she'd fallen asleep and was about to tease her about leaving the dishes to the old folks, but Gabrielle had the look that Maureen thought she had left behind in Gainesville. She was wearing a coat. Maureen put down the pot. "Gabi? What is it?"

"I'm going to go for a walk, Mom. Just let it be."

"I don't think that's a good idea." Maureen caught herself. "Gabrielle. It's dark, foggy, and awfully cold. Can't it wait until morning?"

"Mom." Gabrielle turned from the door.

Maureen's heart caught.

"I need to think."

"Can't you talk with us about it?"

"No. Not now. It's just a very personal …" She stopped, tears gathering in her eyes. "Don't get me wrong. I've had such a wonderful time here. Everyone's been great. But it's not reality. Everything's different now. I have these times when everything's fine, then I remember that I'm going home, and I have to deal with …" Gabrielle faltered. "I just called Robert and his mother said he couldn't talk to me."

Lisa put down her towel. "I think you two need to be alone." She went into the other room.

"Gabrielle. You know his mother. You're just going to have to deal with this while you get your relationship with Robert back on track."

"She said he's gone, Mom. Gone away to school. Somewhere up north … Oh, I can't take this … not now, not now. He promised me." She held herself, rocking back and forth.

Maureen pried Gabrielle's hands apart where they gripped her stomach, put her arms around her daughter.

"Honey, why can't I help? After all we've been through, what could be that bad?"

Gabrielle looked straight into her mother's eyes. Maureen saw the bottom of the pit there, a place she didn't want to go. She willed time to stand still.

"I'm pregnant, Mom."

Maureen felt the floor of the kitchen drop, as if an earthquake were sliding through the middle of Emania.

Her voice sounded tinny and far away, a voice she hadn't commanded to speak. "The hospital said they took care of that. They always do." She held on tighter. "They said they took care of it."

Gabrielle pulled away. She looked at Maureen as if she were a total stranger. Even her tone of voice belonged to someone else. "Mom, what does that have to do with anything?"

"Oh, Gabrielle. I just meant maybe you're misjudging your symptoms. Not having a period could be from the trauma. I'm sure of it."

"Mom, I've done the pregnancy test, and I've been to a doctor."

Maureen held onto Gabrielle's hands, trying to digest the information.

"Mom?" Gabrielle held up their hands, bloodless, locked together.

"Oh, honey, I'm sorry." She let go.

"It's OK. I planned to talk to you and Aunt Lisa tonight, before we went back. I was going to tell you how Robert had promised to marry me." Her voice was that of an old woman.

"Gabrielle, then it's Robert's child?" She stopped at Gabrielle's look. "Of course," she continued, that voice refusing to shut up. "You were together right up until … until it happened," she finished lamely.

"Yes, it's Robert's child. What did you think?" Gabrielle sat heavily on a kitchen chair.

Maureen felt like she should be wearing black. "There's a way out of this, Gabrielle, you'll see."

"Way out? I'm not looking for a way out." Her voice rose shrill and hysterical out into the room.

Brigit appeared beside Gabrielle, her arms reaching out to her. "It will be fine, you'll see. Now that you've said it aloud, it will be fine."

"You knew?"

"When we did the massage. All the signs were there. I thought you were at least three months along."

Maureen's voice was anguished. "Why didn't I see it? She's my child."

"I'm trained to see it, Maureen. Signs can be subtle, especially if the mother wants them to be." She turned to Gabrielle. "The question is, what to do."

"There's nothing to do," Gabrielle said, looking at them both as if they were crazy. "Mom, I've just got to figure this out. I called Robert, and his mom said he didn't want to talk to me. It just didn't seem possible that he wouldn't want to talk to me. If I can just get through to him . . ." She shook her head. "I wanted to go for a walk, that's all." She turned to Brigit. "Besides, I'm Catholic. We don't *do* anything," she said, looking at Maureen. "Isn't that right, Mom?"

Maureen stiffened. She hadn't known how much Gabrielle's religion meant to her. Why not? It was what she had held on to after Dylan died. Maureen remembered little Gabi demanding to go to Sunday school, riding with the neighbors when Maureen couldn't make herself go.

She looked over at Gabrielle. Obviously she'd talked to her father and grandmother about her religious beliefs. She sighed. What else had she missed in her self-absorption? Robert? A man-child, totally under the dominance of his mother. Maureen had been certain he and her daughter had not been intimate, and that as soon as Gabrielle went off to school she would see his lack of maturity. Was it possible for the human mind to invent a relationship to keep from dealing with reality? She heard a voice.

"Mom? Mom, it's OK. I didn't really know how I felt about abortion until I started thinking about it in relation to me." She crossed her hands over her stomach. "Grandmother says babies have a soul as soon as the egg and the sperm get together." She shivered.

The fire had gone out, the candles gutted. The room was chill. Maureen felt icy. "You told Eleanor?"

"C'mon, Mom. I talked to her about a made-up friend of mine. Dad came in and he said the same thing. That's when they started talking about you and how you were going off the deep end with this Pagan stuff."

Brigit stifled a smile.

Gabrielle turned away. "I don't want to talk about this anymore tonight. I just want to go for a walk."

"Do you mind company?" Brigit asked. "I'd kind of like to stretch my legs after all that food."

Maureen understood. Brigit was familiar with the territory. Gabrielle would be safe.

"We'll leave your mom here to get the fire going again."

"Sure, that's fine."

Maureen could tell Gabrielle wanted to be alone, but her good manners kept her from saying no to Brigit. She winged a thank you heavenward. After all they'd been through. She shivered again at the thought of the walled in hole just behind the house. Maureen sat at the kitchen table, her head in her hands. Wasn't it enough? Hadn't they had enough?

She had a panicky desire to call Bryan. She'd talked to him earlier at Miranda's house just as they sat down to dinner. She could tell other people were in the room as he told her how Orlando was beautiful, the weather was beautiful, Miranda's parents were kind and dinner looked delicious. She had hung up the phone, glad that Bryan was happy. At least Miranda's family seemed normal!

She'd called Jason, but there was no answer. She left a happy Thanksgiving message on the machine for him and her mother.

Lisa's cool palm stroked the back of her neck. "Oh, Maureen. I'm so sorry."

Maureen lifted her head. Lisa's eyes were red. Maureen hugged her. "I don't think I have any tears left, Lisa. I just don't know what to do."

"Daylight, Maureen. Wait for daylight."

Maureen shook her head. "This one is going to take more than that, Sis. She's in total denial. I know Robert's family and Robert. She'll lose."

*****

That night, Maureen lay in the twin bed listening to Gabrielle's even breathing. Each knew the other was awake but pretended otherwise. Maureen tried to imagine a rainbow around herself and her daughter as she'd learned during meditation class. She pictured rose-colored air drawn deep into her lungs, exhaled it to curl around Gabrielle's body, cradling her in peace. Gabrielle's breathing grew deeper until, finally, Maureen knew she slept. She turned on her side, still holding her daughter in her mind. Gradually, the image of Gabrielle faded and Dylan appeared, suspended in the dark waters of the cave. He was trying to talk to her but she couldn't hear him, couldn't move in the dream as he slowly curled in on himself and became smaller. Then, as if in a slow-motion scene in a movie, she saw him again, tiny and defenseless, floating in the body of her daughter.

Chapter Fifteen

"Those flowers will wear themselves out by New Year's at this rate," Lisa said, grabbing a piece of turkey from the pan resting on the counter as she looked out the door. "Ouch, hot!" She dropped the meat. "Shouldn't we be having a cookout instead?"

"I suggested it, believe me. No one thought it was appropriate for Christmas. And the name is bougainvillea," Maureen added, pointing to the deep pink blossoms pouring over the fence.

Bryan and Daniel, Bryan's friend from school, sat silent on the patio, their faces raised to the sun like the poinsettias flaring from their pots. Jason practiced putting on the grassy area by the garage.

"I will never get used to a Christmas tree in this weather, no matter how long I live in Florida," Maureen said, turning to the stove.

"You know, it's much more appropriate here. Jesus was born in the summer in a desert country," Gabrielle put in, sprinkling marshmallows on the sweet potato casserole. "He probably saw some of the same flowers we're looking at now."

"Did they have Christmas trees and turkeys then?" Lisa asked innocently.

"And what about all those presents?" added Maureen.

"The Three Kings did set a precedent there, Mom. But I give on the others. I never could win when you and Aunt Lisa joined forces."

"And don't you forget it!" Lisa laughed, hugging her niece hard. "When's Eleanor going to get here, Maureen?"

"I told her dinner at three. She and Donald went to eleven-thirty Mass so they should be here any minute."

"Have you met Donald yet, Aunt Lisa?"

"Nope. Your mom tells me he's really nice, though. What do you think of him?"

"He's different than Grandmother's usual men friends. Older, for one thing. I think there's something going on there. Mom does, too."

Maureen nodded as she stirred broth into the gravy. "We've only been together a couple of times, but I'd say this one's a keeper."

"Wonders never cease," Lisa said, the pain in her voice muffled as she turned on the mixer to whip cream for the pies. They didn't hear the door open, but the smell of Eleanor's perfume overwhelmed the turkey as she and Donald came into the kitchen. She kissed the air by Lisa's cheek, introducing Donald to her almost in passing. She patted Maureen and proceeded out back like the Queen of Sheba. Through the window, Maureen watched her perform the proper introductions. She caught Lisa's look and they both giggled. "You say first," she demanded.

"Say what?" Lisa asked, all innocence as she lifted the beaters from the bowl.

Maureen sighed. "You never admit to your bad thoughts. I always go first. But this time, I'll hold out until the Fourth of July if I have to."

Lisa licked the cream off of one beater and handed the other to Maureen. "We aren't really her daughters," she whispered, putting the bowl of cream in the refrigerator. "We're foundlings. Grandma told me she got us in the cabbage patch."

Maureen struggled to keep a straight face, then hooted out loud. "She really did tell us that, didn't she? When we asked where we came from?"

Bryan peered through the back door. "Mom? Are you OK?"

Maureen wiped her eyes and struggled to straighten her face. "Sure, honey. Ask your dad to come in and carve the cabbage, will you?"

"The cabbage?"

Lisa stepped in as Maureen dissolved into helpless tears. "She means the turkey, dear. It's been a long day."

*****

At precisely three o'clock, Maureen looked around the laden table at her family. "Jason, will you say the blessing?"

As he recited the Catholic grace, Maureen flashed back to Oregon and Gabrielle's wish. It had certainly come true, Jason and Maureen anchoring the table, the family arrayed up one side and down the other. Her heart swelled as she examined the delicate profile of her daughter. Next year there would be a grandchild. Next to Gabrielle, Lisa smiled back at her. She had been seeing Jerome. Who knew where that would lead. The family continued to grow and gather here.

Gabrielle spoke up. "I'd like to give thanks for my family and this place where we always know we can come home."

Bryan added a hearty "Amen. And for the world's greatest cook and mother, a special Amen."

"I'd like to add something," Daniel said, "if it's all right?"

"We'd be honored," Maureen answered.

"I would like to ask the blessings of the gods on this family and on families all over the world who are not so fortunate."

Maureen saw her mother's eyebrows raise to her hairline, a sign they had dreaded as children.

"So appropriate, my dear, to remember the less fortunate on this day. Thank you for reminding us. And I would like to ask a special blessing on the one who makes all of this possible, our dear Jason."

"Well, then, let's eat it before it gets cold, shall we?" Jason responded, his face pink with pleasure.

"Here, here." Donald lifted his glass of ice-water in a toast.

Maureen sensed relief flooding her heart as she suddenly accepted that Donald loved her mother. She hadn't realized that a fear existed deep down inside her that she would have to care for Eleanor and Eleanor would hate it. She looked at Donald. He certainly looked healthy! She blushed as his eyes met hers, and she was convinced he could read her mind. He smiled and nodded down the table.

*****

The dishes were done and Jason had taken the heartier of the group on a hike along the Bayshore. As the door closed behind Eleanor and Donald, off to visit friends they'd met on their latest cruise, Maureen sat in the backyard. She inhaled the smell of blossoms on the grapefruit tree, the marvelous tree that bloomed twice a year, no matter what. It would bloom again in March, and they would have small and large fruit on the tree at the same time. Even in the trees there are rebels, she mused to herself. Those who choose to do their thing in their own time. She sighed, pulling her sweater closer.

"May I join you?"

She started at the soft voice of Daniel. "Of course." She pushed a chair across the patio with her foot. "You didn't join the Spartans?"

He chuckled. "I started to, but I really wanted a chance to visit with you a little." He sat, his slight frame enveloped in the wicker rocker. The whites of his eyes shone in the early moonlight, his dark skin blurring against the house. "I really thank you for letting me spend the holiday with your family. When Bryan heard I wasn't going anywhere, he insisted you wouldn't mind."

Maureen pushed her rocker gently with her foot. "He knows I don't. You're welcome, anytime." Daniel looked a little older than Bryan, and she realized that with the preparations for Christmas, she hadn't asked anything at all about him.

"How did you meet my son?"

"I'm Bryan's teacher. I'm working on my doctorate in Philosophy, and I teach his Western Civ class."

"You seem so young to be teaching at the university."

"I graduated ahead of my class in Honolulu and got lucky. They accepted me just as I was about to give up and go to work on my parents' plantation."

"Their what?"

"Plantation. My folks have a pineapple farm. They're mortified to have a son who wants to be a philosopher, but at the same time, they're kind of proud. My dad never got through high school."

"I don't believe I've ever met someone who was actually a native of Hawaii. Has your family been there long?"

"Four generations. I'll be going back when I finish, if I can get a job.

Hawaii is a beautiful place." He halted his rocker. "Not that Florida isn't, but Hawaii is home."

"No offense, Daniel. Though I do believe this time of year, I love Florida as much as if I was born here. What does a philosopher do to get a job?"

"Teach, Mrs. Manley. That's about it in the job market right now. What I'm really interested in is … I'm sorry. I was about to pontificate!"

"No, I'd really like to know," Maureen said, and she was telling the truth.

"Well, I'm interested in bringing the feminine principles into the workplace. That's what my dissertation will be about."

"The feminine principles? Is that really workable, Daniel?"

"Well, risky is one of the nicest words they've used so far, but they're kind of intrigued at the university because I'm a minority male writing about something as esoteric as spirituality in the corporate structure. Sounds weird even to me sometimes." He laughed, a pleasant sound floating through the night air.

Maureen thought of the blessing Daniel had added at dinner. "Will parts of your dissertation deal with the more primitive idea of the spiritual?"

"Primitive?"

"Um. Bad choice of words. The beliefs of people prior to the one-god culture. How's that?"

"Much better. Yes, that's one of the areas I'm working in." He struggled for words. "I think that unless we bring the spirit and heart back to the corporate world, we're doomed. It's not a very popular notion in Western culture."

"In nearly any culture, Daniel. You're embarked on a huge selling job." Maureen leaned closer and looked at her son's friend in the light of the rising moon. "You know, I believe you're on to something. You may be before your time, but you're on to something. I'd appreciate it if you'd let me know how it's going."

"I'd be happy to. Actually, I'd like your point of view. Bryan tells me you're a teacher and very astute. He also says you're open to new ideas, even if they're old ideas."

"Bryan is prejudiced. Actually, I'm just substitute teaching right now, trying to find my way back in. It used to be satisfying when I taught music, but it's been a long time and lots of things have changed."

Daniel cleared his throat. "Your daughter is very lovely. Is she also interested in what you call the old-new ideas?"

Perhaps it was only conversation, but Maureen felt the intensity of this young man behind his question, and she felt another thing. Safety. He was a harbor for her daughter, not a threat. She wondered how much Daniel knew about Gabrielle, choosing her words carefully. "My daughter had a hard year. She's back in school here at the University of South Florida. Her troubles seem to have led her more into orthodoxy or the old-old ideas. But you'd be better off to ask her."

"Ask who?" Gabrielle came into the back yard with a glass of orange juice in her hand.

"Daniel was asking about your school," Maureen answered. "Did you know he was getting his doctorate?"

"Bryan told me." She sat in the chair next to Daniel. "Bryan says you're very smart."

Maureen could feel the heat from his face all the way to her chair.

"Smart is relative. I work hard and I like what I do. Do you also like what you do?"

"Sometimes. I changed my major from teaching to nursing, and I'll probably stay with it, but this is my last semester for a while. I'll have plenty of time to make up my mind."

"Bryan tells me you're going out to visit your aunt in California?"

"Actually, I'm going to work in a center in Oregon while I have my child."

Maureen heard Daniel's indrawn breath. "I didn't know you were married. Congratulations."

"I accept the congratulations, but I'm not married."

The silence thickened. "Would anyone like anything to drink while I'm in the kitchen?" Maureen asked.

"Yes, please Mrs. Manley. Some water would be nice."

When Maureen returned to the backyard, Gabrielle and Daniel were deep in conversation. She set the water on the table next to his hand and went back in the house. The universe worked in mysterious ways.

*****

Maureen toweled off after her shower and slathered herself with the Chanel body lotion her mother had given her for Christmas. She put on the new robe she'd gotten from Jason and gave herself a good look in the mirror. The robe was silk, black with creamy lilies. Maybe she had endowed the gift with more meaning than he had intended, but she and Jason had not had sex since before she went to Oregon, and this robe was not a bathrobe. It was definitely a bedroom robe. She was tired after the long day, but her nerves were buzzing. Gabrielle and Daniel had stayed out in the garden long after the rest of the household had settled. Bryan teased Daniel about preferring the company of his sister before he left to go to Ybor City with some of his old friends. She ran her fingers through her hair and felt the tingle of electricity. If she was going to stay in this marriage, sooner or later the physical part had to resume. She was in the full heart of her life, unwilling to be a nun. It was almost a new year. What better time? Jason was usually quite mellow on Christmas, once the hoopla was done. Looking around the table at his family gave him a great sense of satisfaction. Maureen took a deep breath and went into the bedroom.

Jason was propped up in bed, not asleep as she had feared. She had read him right. She inhaled one more time, breathing in thoughts of union, the bonds of husband and wife and family, breathing out judgement of the past. It was hard, but she was working on it diligently. Jason's gaze traveled down her body from the open neck of her robe to her bare feet. She hadn't put on a gown, and the silk skimmed her body like skin. She felt the pulse in her neck quicken, and she breathed a prayer of thanks. She had thought she would never feel desire again. She neared the bed, the steady heat of a banked fire radiating from her.

"Do you know where our daughter is?" Jason asked, the eyes she had thought caressing, accusing.

Maureen hit her leg on the foot of the bed and caught herself as she sat heavily on the mattress. She couldn't speak.

"She's down there in the garden with that boy."

"Daniel?"

"Who else? What was Bryan thinking of to bring him here?"

Maureen's brain whirled in confusion. "I don't know what you're saying, Jason. Daniel seems a very nice, young man." What in the world was happening? Maybe Jason thought the pregnancy was to be kept secret. Maybe he thought Daniel would find out and be shocked.

"She's told him about her pregnancy, Jason. He seemed very accepting of her. I think he'll be a good friend ..."

"He's ..." Jason stopped, visibly controlling himself. "He's colored, for God's sake Maureen. Haven't we got enough problems?"

Maureen's head reeled. She moved from the bed to her chair near the window and propped her throbbing leg onto the ottoman.

"This will not happen in my house, Maureen. I've put up with a lot, but I'm drawing the line."

"What won't happen, Jason? I'm lost."

"You are, but the kids aren't. Yet. I don't want Bryan bringing that person here again, and you need to tell him."

A vision of Jerome came into Maureen's mind. Jerome and Lisa. It had seemed so natural to her. How often did she need to be reminded that the world was a different place than the one she desired with all her heart? Jason wasn't a bad person, and that made it all so much more terrible. He really believed he was right. She struggled to find words.

"I won't do that Jason. It's my house, too, and I've always thought the kids were free to bring home anyone they saw fit. I can't agree with this."

"You don't have to agree. I won't have it. I work to pay the bills, I don't get much in return. Even you would have to agree with that. Your mother agrees ..."

"You discussed this with my mother?" Maureen's voice rose hysterically, then she remembered Lisa in the next room and forced herself to breathe deeply. She tried again. "Just what did you and Eleanor discuss?"

"The fact that I needed to take back my role as man of the house. Let's face it, Maureen. These past few months you've really gone off the deep end. We've been patient, but now your attitude is affecting the kids. Fine, Gabi's going off to Oregon to have the baby. That's good for her, but I don't want her getting indoctrinated with that stuff you nearly fell for. Donald's handled adoptions in his practice, and he says he can help her when the time comes."

"Slow down, Jason. You've run over me and around me, and I have to take this one step at a time." She imagined warm rose light surrounding her. Gradually it seeped into her bones, straightening her back, warming her cramping leg. "First of all, have you talked to Gabrielle about this adoption thing? She told me she wanted to keep the baby."

"That's what she says now, but we have time to talk some sense into her."

"What if I think she's made the right decision?"

Jason snorted. "That wouldn't surprise me." He made a visible effort to control himself. "Look, Maureen. She's not finished with school, she has her whole life ahead of her. Besides, this baby ..." He stopped, a palpable look of revulsion crossing his face. "This is not our grandchild. It's the child of a rapist and attempted murderer. We'll do what's right by the Church but that's it."

"Jason, this is Gabrielle's child, our blood. When it is born, like it or not, it is our grandchild." Maureen looked at this stranger who had been her husband. How had this happened? Five minutes earlier she had been prepared to love him and now this. She felt cracking in the air, a literal disintegration of this sad relationship.

"We have plenty of time to talk to Gabi about this. Right now, I want you to back me up when I tell Bryan not to bring this Daniel person home again. He's got his eye on our daughter."

"He's only talking to her, Jason." Maureen felt her voice reasoning as with a child.

"The only way for the colored people of this world to raise themselves up is to marry white people. I'm not going to let that happen."

Maureen caught her breath. "Jason, who have you been talking to? This can't be you."

"Obviously you've been more concerned with your friends than with me, or you'd know it *is* me. You just never really cared what I thought."

Maureen leaned carefully against the back of the chair. Was he telling the truth? Had she been so concerned with herself and the kids that she hadn't paid attention to him? He was like a plant that had grown into some unexpected form in the back of the yard, unobserved. But now he was telling her who he was. She had better listen carefully.

"I always cared, Jason, but you're probably right. Neither of us saw what was going on with the other one. We were too busy pretending everything was the way it should be."

"That's just more of that psycho babble you brought home with you. You weren't like that when I married you. You wanted the same things I did."

Maureen felt the confusion in him radiating around the room. No, not confusion, exactly. More like betrayal.

She tried to moderate her voice. "What things, Jason?"

"A home, family, normalcy for Christ's sake!"

"And we had none of those?"

Jason drew in his breath in the dark of their bedroom, the dull glow of the bathroom lamp cutting across his face. And she swore she felt the evil thing let loose in the room before it left his mouth, before it flew across the bed and entered her heart.

"Not after you let Dylan die."

It was said. After sixteen years of silent accusation, it was said. Maureen was cut loose, adrift in evil. It was strange, but she knew the color of evil now. It was a brownish green, like water stirring up a mud bottom, water filled with trash and litter that sucked and swirled down until you couldn't fight any more, gave up to its power. The thing about this particular evil was that she knew where it came from, and the source was her husband, the man who said he would cherish her until death parted them. She heard him over her, heard him saying "I'm, sorry, I didn't mean it, I'm just so frustrated." But she kept moving away and then she saw the water turning clear again, a sparkling aquamarine, and there were beautiful sleek seals circling and playing and in their midst was Dylan and his eyes sought hers and his love shot straight to her soul and she knew what she had to do.

Chapter Sixteen

She came back to Jason sitting on the floor next to her chair, his head in his hands, and the possibility of tears glinting between his fingers. She put her hand on his head.

"I forgive you Jason, but I will never forget the things you've said to me tonight because you really meant them."

He shook his head. "No, not the last one. I don't know why I said it."

"Because you've thought it, Jason, and you have to live with that. Besides, meaning the rest of them was bad enough. We're two different people now, not the two young innocents who married all those years ago. We had a reason for being together. I'm not sure what it was but probably the children."

Jason got up from the floor. "I suppose you're going to tell me there was a reason for Dylan, too." His voice was sharp and derisive.

"Some day he'll tell us why he chose us for parents, but I don't have an answer for that. I really think we need to sleep on all of this and, when the holiday is over, decide what we want to do about it.

"You'd dump all we've worked for—the family, everything—just because we're different people? Lots of marriages survive that."

"That's true. But I want more than that. For myself and for you, too." She was stunned at the tenderness she felt for this man who had just flung her into the abyss. Her lack of anger seemed to stir him to even more violent words, but she knew it was what he was losing that had him reaching for anything to get to her. He knew she had made up her mind, and that he would not know what to do without her. "Jason, let's stop this. We'll talk tomorrow. And about Bryan and Daniel? You'll have to talk to them yourself. It is your house, and I respect whatever rules you want to lay down in this house. I just won't be here to follow them because I can't." She gathered up her pillow and blanket and went to the door.

"Where are you going?" he hissed into the dark.

"I'll sleep in the guest room with Lisa."

"What are people going to think? Don't you care about anybody but yourself?"

"Jason, people will think what they will. The same as you do." She closed the door quietly behind her and felt the slight shudder as his pillow hit the door.

Two days after Christmas, Maureen took Lisa to the airport.

"You're coming out with Gabrielle?"

"For sure, now. There's nothing to hold me here, except Bryan. And he has his own life."

"I won't ask what happened, Maureen, but I can't wait until the two of you come." She looked pensive.

"What is it, Lisa?"

"Jerome wants to marry me."

"Lisa! I wondered when you'd finally do it." She glanced over at her sister as they sat at a stoplight near Tampa International.

"I'm just not sure. We're so happy the way we are, and we're good friends."

"Lisa, I can't tell you what to do. Obviously you're gun shy anyway after your experience with 'what's his name.' I guess the color issue isn't exactly small, either."

"Well, I don't expect Eleanor to congratulate me, if that's what you mean. But it's the age thing. I just can't get past it."

"Look, you'll know when it's right. Trust yourself. I don't think he's going anywhere. As for Eleanor, she and Jason both live lives that exclude so much, and we can't change that. The rest of us will be there no matter what."

"I know that, Sis. Thanks."

Maureen watched as the plane lifted her sister into the air and headed for California. How she missed her when she was gone. She already looked forward to the trip out with Gabrielle.

Maureen kept busy cleaning up from Christmas and going through her closet for winter clothes she would need in Oregon. Gabrielle's baby, her grandchild, was due in May, but Brigit wanted Maureen there as soon as possible to help set up the program for spring. Robert's parents had sent him to a private college in Maine, and Gabrielle seemed resigned to single parenthood. She'd be lucky if she got her hands on the baby at Emania with all the mothering women there. She interrupted her packing to take Bryan back to Gainesville. Daniel had gone on earlier to prepare for his classes. Jason was at work when Maureen and Bryan left. They were both quiet for the first few miles.

"You'll miss Aunt Lisa, won't you, Mom," Bryan said, a statement not a question.

"Like my right arm," she answered. "But I'm going out to see her soon. I'm glad we have this time to talk. I need your advice."

Bryan snorted.

"No kidding, Bryan. You know I always value your opinion."

"I know, Mom. But these last few months have been ... I don't even have the words for it. From August to the end of December, it might as well have been five years as five months. I don't think I know anything about anything."

"You've been so strong. My god, Bryan, you saved your sister's life! I've been going around on crutches and muttering to myself, and you went back to school and got on with your life."

"Maybe I just don't show it like you and Gabi ... shit. I mean Gabrielle."

"I know, it's hard on all of us."

"That's a platitude, Mom."

"No, no. I meant saying Gabrielle, not your mental anguish over the past few months. Surely you didn't think I would make light of that?"

"I didn't want to add to your stuff, and Dad's not exactly receptive. He's the one who buries things!"

"I know, Bryan, but it's always been his way, and I don't think he's going to change."

"Mom, hang on. The Wildwood exit is coming up. How about Dairy Queen?"

"Oh man, I've just been making my New Year's resolutions."

"But you have two more days. Let's do it. Hot fudge. Yum."

"Do you think I could have it and be skinny like you?"

"Not likely. Why would you want to be anyway?" She felt his eyes appraise her. "Daniel says you're the best looking mom he's seen."

The heat nearly suffocated her. And she'd taken her herbs that morning. She heard Bryan's wonderful laugh, a long dormant sound.

"You can't help blushing. That's why we like to tease you."

A few minutes later they were sitting on a picnic table, licking the rapidly melting ice cream off the sides of the cones.

"I wonder if people up North are eating ice cream three days after Christmas," Maureen mused, her face turned up toward the sun.

"So, what is it you want to talk to me about?"

Maureen wasn't caught off guard. Bryan had always come directly to the point whenever it occurred to him.

"For one thing, I was a little concerned that you weren't quite ready to go back to school. Are things going OK for you?"

"Oh, yeah. I just wanted to see how you were doing, and we don't have much time together. And," he hesitated, fumbling for the words, then shrugged. "It seems that Daniel's appointed me his spokesman."

"His spokesman? I thought it was strange that he left a day earlier than you. He said something about classes, but it sounded contrived."

"He wants to see more of Gabrielle, and he wanted me to test the water."

"Christmas day I would have asked you why, but I've been educated since."

"You talked to Dad?"

"Oh, Bryan." Maureen tossed the limp cone into a trash bin. "I should have talked to you first. Then maybe I wouldn't have been so shocked."

"You always want to think the best of people, Mom. Dad was bound to object. At least now I know it's official when I talk to Daniel."

"It's up to him and Gabrielle, not your father. I really like what I saw of him, and I think she did, too. It's hard to tell right now. She's just starting to come around, and with the baby …"

"Well, I told him the same thing, but he's kind of old-fashioned. Wanted your blessing to 'court' her, for Pete's sake."

"I love that word. Don't you pick on him, Bryan."

"You forget who brought him home?"

Maureen hugged her son. "You're one of the good guys, Bryan. Are you sure you don't want to talk to me about anything else?"

"Mom, I really am fine."

"I know you're strong, Bryan, but what you've been through is not normal or easy. I know how I get eaten up with guilt, especially if I think I'm responsible for something …" Her voice trailed off.

"Do you think I should feel responsible for what happened to Gabrielle?" Anguish painted his voice like a bruise.

"Of course not, but I didn't listen when people told me the same things about Dylan and then about Gabi. I thought maybe you were struggling with the same things."

"I did feel that way. I tried to talk to the counselors at school, but they were so burned out from the murders, a rape didn't seem quite important enough. Then I met Daniel. We talked for hours, even about Dylan." He looked at her carefully. "That was a subject we didn't discuss in our family, you know."

"I know, Bryan. And I regret that more than just about anything else. Anytime you want to, I'm ready."

"Daniel's background really helped me. Maybe I needed to talk to him before I talked to you. He believes everything has a reason. He's a great guy. We're talking about working together on his ideas. I hope Gabrielle likes him. He'd be really good for her."

"I think she already does, honey. And Daniel told me about some of his work. I'd be so proud if you were involved."

"I know you would, Mom. Miranda says whatever I want is what she wants, too. You'll like her."

"If you chose her, I will. You both have a long way to go with school and life, but ..." She broke off at his look. "Right, more than you asked for." She smiled at her lovely son. "Let's go. I want to get to Gainesville in time to have dinner at Skeeters."

"You're joking! I don't eat that stuff anymore."

Maureen almost slammed the car door on her foot. "Did I hear right?"

It was Bryan's turn to blush. "Daniel's a health nut. I guess he just wore me down."

"Well then, you take me to dinner."

"Done. Now, what's going on with you that you haven't had the guts to tell me yet?"

Maureen took a breath as she entered I-75 and headed north. "I'm going out to Oregon with Gabrielle."

"I thought you would. I can't see her having her baby without you."

"Not just that. I think I may be going permanently." She waited for his reaction.

"You're leaving Dad?"

She couldn't tell from his voice. There was absolutely no clue. She nodded. "I've told you some about my trip there, but there's a lot more."

"Is there someone else you want to be married to?" Bryan's voice had taken on a childlike quality. She felt a little stirring of doubt under her skin.

"That's not it, Bryan. It's just that I found a part of me out there I didn't even know existed." Maureen thought of Emania, the fire, the women, Dylan. "I'm going to tell you all of it, Bryan. Then you'll know for yourself why I want to go back."

It was nearly a half hour before she concluded, even without the part about Stephen. She had glossed that over, but Bryan was too tuned into her.

"And this guy, Stephen? You don't want to be with him?"

"I did, but I left and told him I had to make it work with your dad for all our sakes. I didn't realize how dead our marriage really was."

"But he's still there, right?"

"No. He went to France."

"But you still want to go."

"Brigit called me. She has so many people coming for the spring and summer sessions that she wants to train me to help. She thinks I'm a natural."

Bryan was quiet on his side of the car, looking out the window.

"Gabrielle will have her baby there, then we'll all decide what to do after that." She laid a tentative hand on her son's arm. "I just can't imagine living on the other side of the country from you!"

"It'll give me a great new place to visit." Bryan turned toward her. "You can't plan your life around us anymore, Mom. Who knows? I might go to Hawaii or Alaska. Do you think I should stay here so I won't miss you?"

"Of course not! I've always told you to go and do what you want ..." He'd trapped her. Maureen smiled. "Done in again by Bryan's brain."

"I feel really bad about Dad, but he seems happy just like he is."

"You think your dad is happy?"

"In his own way, yeah. He isn't like us, Mom. He doesn't want to wrestle with cosmic questions. And he shouldn't have to."

"Like I said, I should have talked to you earlier."

"You always fit yourself into his image of what you should be. Nobody should have to do that, though we liked it at the time. It was nice having all of us together."

"Your dad used to be different, Bryan. When Dylan died, he took Dad's light with him. He never got it back. Besides, his way of avoiding the truth can go on, while mine came to a screeching halt the day you guys left for school." She watched the stream of northern cars heading for Tampa and points south. "Your dad can't change, Bryan."

"Mom, he doesn't want to. That's why I say he's happy. You may be right about Dylan, but the dad I've known has always been this way. Maybe you just wished he was different."

They stayed busy with their own thoughts until Maureen pulled into the apartment parking lot.

"Mom?"

She turned off the engine.

"Won't it be hard not to have somebody? I mean somebody who, you know, puts their arm around you? Stuff like that?"

"Bryan." She leaned over and hugged him. "Your dad and I haven't had that in many years. I get warmth from family and friends, not your dad. But, yes, in all honesty. It would be nice."

Bryan got out of the car and Maureen heard him mumble. She stuck her head out. "What?"

He opened the trunk. "I said I wonder where Dad gets warmth."

EPILOGUE

It was nearly New Year's, a year later. Maureen sat in front of the fire, the golden lights of the Christmas tree sparking off the red and green balls. The air smelled of pine and cinnamon. Tomorrow they would plant the living tree between the cliff and the studio. She was rereading a letter from Bryan while the apple pies she was making for supper finished baking. She couldn't wait to see him on his spring break. She skipped through the greeting part.

"… and I think I've decided to go to Law School. I'll major in political science starting next semester. Dad says maybe it's time to add someone to the firm with a public service eye. He says it's the 'thing of the future.' Daniel agrees, but neither of us sees me doing this in Dad's firm. Oh, we talked about this over dinner at the club Christmas day, just Dad, Patsy, Grandmother and Donald. I'm sure you've heard about Patsy from Grandmother. Dad's been seeing her for a couple of months, and according to him, she's one heck of a golfer and not bad at tennis either. I guess when your divorce is final, they'll get married. They're talking about buying a place on the golf course after Dad sells our house. I assume you know all this, since it's your house, too."

Maureen dropped the letter in her lap. Their house with a new family. It felt odd but good. She tried to imagine Patsy, but everything she came up with was such a stereotype she was ashamed. She was relieved that Jason had moved on so quickly. She had suffered enormous guilt about leaving him.

She straightened her glasses and read on.

"Grandmother and Donald are going on a cruise to Alaska next summer. I told them you were practically on the way. Have you heard from them?"

She looked down on the quilt where her granddaughter napped and smiled. The baby had worn herself out crawling backward all morning. Gabrielle and Daniel should be back from their walk any minute. Having them here for the holidays had been wonderful.

Yes, she's heard from her mother and Donald. Neither they, nor Jason, had come to Oregon for Gabrielle's wedding, but the note from her mother had mentioned her desire to see her great-granddaughter. Maureen picked up the wedding picture from the coffee table. What a beautiful day that had been. She closed her eyes.

*****

It had been sparkling, the best the coast had to offer that April afternoon. Warm for the time of year. The heaters weren't needed in the tent outside, and the Pacific earned its name in the background. Gabrielle, so lovely in a cream cotton gown and sandals, had carried a bouquet of apricot colored roses. They had written their own vows, and Maureen had nearly broken down when Daniel promised to love Gabrielle and her child through this life and into the next. Gabrielle had glowed with happiness and health.

She'd joined her husband in Gainesville when the baby was six months old, leaving her child in Maureen's care while she went to nursing school. Maureen, Brigit and Mary Virginia had shared the summer and fall seminars and the care of Gabrielle's child up until this past week. Maureen hadn't known how she would bear it when Daniel and Gabrielle came to take the baby away. But, as was the norm in their lives, fate had stepped in once again. Daniel's Christmas gift to Maureen was a letter in a beautifully wrapped box, a letter of acceptance for him to teach in Palo Alto, not such a very long way away. And Gabrielle was going to study Therapeutic Touch there. In the summer, she and Daniel would come to Emania, and Gabrielle would teach the rest of the team how to do the healing touch for their clients. She might even teach with them during the summer sessions.

She touched the top of her sleeping grandchild's head. People said she looked just like Gabrielle, but others would point out traces of Daniel around the eyes or maybe in the mouth. Her dark hair that glowed with a hint of auburn in certain light was a combined legacy from Maureen and Jason.

Curled in a comfortable chair across from Maureen, Brigit finished reading her mail as Gabrielle came in, bringing cool mist in her wake. She kissed both women on the cheek, then collapsed on the floor, gazing at her sleeping child. "Where's Aunt Lisa?"

"She and Jerome went to the store. They should be back by dinner."

"I hope so! Jerome and Daniel are designated cooks tonight." She tucked the quilt in around her sleeping child. "I wish Aunt Lisa would stop fighting it and marry Jerome."

"And why is that?" Brigit asked. "They seem fine to me."

"I guess since I'm so happy, I just want everyone else to be, too." She touched her mom gently on the leg. "Looks like you guys had plenty of mail. Any news?"

"I was just rereading Bryan's letter. I do miss him."

"Me too, Mom. I'll be the first one here when he comes in April."

"I have news," Brigit said, waving an airmail letter in front of them.

Maureen's heart caught, a rapid pulse jumping in her neck as she recognized Stephen's handwriting on the envelope.

"Stephen's coming home."

"Stephen? I get to meet the legendary Stephen? I saw some of his art in San Francisco. He's incredible. Mom?" She looked up at Maureen from the floor. "Have you seen any of his work except for what's here in the studio?"

"No, just what I saw last year." Last year, she thought. It seemed eons ago. So much had happened since then it was impossible to think about.

Gabrielle's voice interrupted her reverie. "All of his women reminded me of something, but I couldn't figure it out."

"Well, he'll be here next month."

"Did he say why he's coming home, Brigit?" Maureen asked, her voice wavering as it struggled through her tight throat.

Brigit looked down at the paper and put on her reading glasses. "He says the light just wasn't quite right over there."

"I thought the light was wonderful in France," Gabrielle said, her voice puzzled. "I can't imagine leaving there."

"He says here that it lacked a certain component, something to do with Titian." Brigit looked up. Maureen's red-gold hair flared in the light of the fire.

Perhaps it was only her imagination, but as her granddaughter opened her eyes and looked directly at her, she felt as if time had condensed in this one space and that everyone she ever loved or ever knew was in this room. Lisa came in the door, the tips of her hair glittering with moisture, the laughter spilling from her mouth like a waterfall. Jerome and Daniel were close behind her, cold air lifting from their clothes, warming in the light of the fire.

"Well, it's about time," Gabrielle crooned, picking up her child and holding her like an offering. "Look, Lynda, everyone's home."

Not quite, Maureen thought, but enough to be grateful for. She quickly said a prayer of thanks that everyone was healthy, and for now, life was good.

She heard Jerome and Daniel in the kitchen, laying out supper plans as if they were about to attempt to climb the Matterhorn. The smell of pies ready to be taken from the oven wafted into the room under the buzzing of the timer. She roused herself to take the pies out of the oven.

"I'll get them, Mom," Gabrielle said, "if you'll take Lynda for a while."

"Tough decision," Maureen laughed, holding out her arms. Gabrielle handed her the wiggling, freshly diapered little girl who would be the first vessel for her mother's stories. In the meantime, Maureen would tell her the ones she knew, and Daniel would add the ones he knew and so on. And maybe someday, if they were lucky, Lynda's great-grandmother would offer up the things that only she could share before it was too late. Maureen looked into the gray-green eyes of this human link in her family necklace, and she knew, without a doubt, that she would do it all again, even knowing what she knew now. It was worth the pain to feel this joy.

"Once upon a time," she began, as her granddaughter snuggled her sleek little head into the hook of Maureen's arm, "there lived a family of seals."

Time slid away as the briny scent of the sea filled the room, and Maureen felt her skin soften to the texture of the child in her arms. Once again she was swimming with Dylan in the warm, turquoise liquid womb of the universe.